Shattered Destiny

James W. Swanson

Published by James Swanson, 2023.

This is a work of fiction. Similarities to real people, places, or events are entirely coincidental.

SHATTERED DESTINY

First edition. September 6, 2023.

ISBN: 979-8223614692

Written by James W. Swanson.

This novel is lovingly dedicated to my wife Karan and my daughters Dawn and Robin for their mega-encouragement and support of my long-standing desire to turn this story into a published novel! Special thanks also to my very smart grandson, Jacob Nelson, for his invaluable help proofreading my manuscript!

Disclaimer

This is a work of fiction. Names, characters, places, and incidents either are the product of the author's imagination or are used fictitiously, and any resemblance to actual persons, living or dead, businesses, companies, events, or locales is unintended and entirely coincidental.

****

Military Acronyms and Terms Used in the Story

Flag Officer – a general or admiral of any of the military services

CSAF – Chief of Staff, the senior military officer in charge of the entire Air Force. Always a four-star general

JAG – generic term for any military lawyer, also known as a judge advocate

JAG Corps – the entire military legal organization of the Air Force

TJAG – the Judge Advocate General, the flag officer in charge of the JAG Corps and primary legal advisor to CSAF.

DJAG – the Deputy to the TJAG

SJA – staff judge advocate, the senior military lawyer at any unit or organizational level of the military

AFB – Air Force Base

TDY – official travel

PROLOGUE

The exquisite tapestry of history is woven in very large part by a quixotic weaver named Chance. It takes no great insight or analysis to understand that a seemingly insignificant "random" event can have an enormously profound cascading impact on how subsequent events unfold over time.

In late March of 1981, John Hinckley, Jr., an obsessed 25-year-old product of an unusually privileged upbringing, bizarrely attempted to win the attention and affections of an impossibly unreachable romantic target, movie star Jodie Foster, by shooting the 40th President of the United States. The attack left Ronald Reagan and three others seriously wounded, though all ultimately survived. The most grievously hurt was James Brady, the colorful and popular press secretary to the new President. As many still remember, one of Hinckley's bullets struck Brady in the temple that tumultuous day – although Brady survived, he did so only at the price of extraordinarily debilitating injuries that persisted though the rest of life and clearly contributed to his death in 2014.

History records that Ronald Reagan quickly recovered (although it was likely a much closer call than we were led to believe at the time) and went on to serve two terms as President of the United States. During those eight years in office, Reagan orchestrated and presided over both a national economic recovery that endured through much of the 1980s and an inarguable reinvigoration of America's armed forces. And – not coincidentally in the view of many – within a decade of Reagan's inauguration, the world had undergone an astonishingly radical transformation which, among other things, saw the disintegration of the Iron Curtain and the chaotic dissolution of the once mighty and menacing Soviet Union. The consequences of that transformation have continued to play out to the present.

It is now well over 40 years since John Hinckley attempted to end the life of President Reagan, and we know with the clarity of hindsight how history has unfolded since that event. But what might have happened in the world if history's fickle weaver had altered just a thread on that rainy Washington day in March 1981? More to point, what if John Hinckley's assassination attempt against Ronald Reagan had succeeded?

CHAPTER 1

Washington, D.C.
2:25 p.m., March 30, 1981

The cheers of the 3,500 AFL-CIO delegates had barely subsided as President Ronald Reagan, two months into the office to which he had been so recently and resoundingly elected, exited through the VIP door of the Washington Hilton. Agent Jerry Parr, head of the White House Secret Service Detail, walked expressionless and alert to the President's right. Twenty-five feet away, Secret Service Agent Timothy McCarthy stood stoically by the open passenger door of the presidential limousine, its engine already running.

To the President's left strode White House Deputy Chief of Staff Michael Deaver. As he stepped into the misty rain behind Deaver, Presidential Press Secretary Jim Brady stopped, suddenly wondering if he'd retrieved — he was always losing things — his lucky silver pen he'd used only minutes before to jot himself a reminder as the President had been speaking.

He paused for no more than two seconds as he reflexively touched his breast pocket. Reassured to feel the pen's hard metallic touch, he resumed walking a little more quickly so as to catch up with Deaver, who was now some six steps ahead of him vectoring toward the staff car third in line behind the Presidential limousine.

Brady noticed two rain-coated DC policemen standing in front of the small group of cordoned reporters to his left. Both had their backs to him, but their heads were turned toward the waving actor-turned-governor-turned-President now just three steps away from the limo's open right rear door.

Without at first understanding what he was watching, Brady saw the older of the two cops fall limp to the pavement at the same time he heard the first firecracker pop. Quickly turning his gaze back to the direction of his walk, he saw Deaver hunker low and step off the curb behind the limo.

Five more rapid pops sounded, and Brady almost thought he felt the air move just in front of his face. His eyes instinctively moved to the door of the limo in time to see Parr roughly push the President inside. As the limo started to screech away, the press secretary watched dumbstruck as Agent McCarthy clutched his belly and fell grotesquely to the sidewalk.

Only then did Brady become aware of the cacophony of shouts, swearing, and screams to his left. Turning his head abruptly toward the noise, he was amazed to see what reminded him of an old fashioned "dog-pile" . . . that was the term kids used for it when he was growing up in Centralia, Illinois . . . just behind the press cordon next to the gray brick wall.

As he began to understand what he had just seen, Brady reflexively imitated Deaver's crouch and ran to the Deputy Chief of Staff's side.

"Holy shit!" exclaimed Brady as he grabbed Deaver's arm and hustled him hastily toward the far side of their still stationary staff car. "Holy shit is right, Bear" panted Deaver in response.

In the now rolling limo, Agent Parr quickly lifted himself off the President, still prone on the floor. Parr's eyes immediately fixated on the bright red oxygenated blood at both corners of Reagan's mouth. Parr gasped as he noticed what at first looked like a patch of wet red hair just above Reagan's left ear. "GW now!" screamed the Agent to the driver.

CHAPTER 2

Washington, D.C.
1:15 a.m., March 31, 1981

It was a somber but composed Dr. Dennis O'Leary, dean of Clinical Affairs and public spokesman for the George Washington University Hospital, who stood at the podium in the auditorium that now served as a makeshift press room. Behind him stood a visibly exhausted James Brady and Dr. Daniel Ruge, the President's personal physician. Every available seat was filled, although a number of seats just in front of the podium had been hastily removed to make room for over two dozen television cameras.

Their unforgiving lights accentuated Brady's way-past-five-o'clock shadow and the enormous bags under his reddened eyes. The throng of reporters hardly stirred as it waited for O'Leary to talk. Looking down at the podium, he collected his thoughts for a few long seconds, then looked up and began to speak.

"As the White House announced several hours ago, President Reagan expired at 4:22 this afternoon . . . I mean yesterday afternoon. I've been asked to provide you with a brief medical summary of what occurred and give the results of the preliminary autopsy that has now been conducted.

"The President arrived unconscious at our emergency room at approximately twenty to three. The receiving physicians quickly determined that he had suffered two separate gunshot wounds, one to the left side of his torso and the other to his head, just above the left ear.

"The President was immediately prepped and taken to surgery, where our team of trauma-trained neural and thoracic surgeons worked for over an hour and a half attempting to stabilize his condition.

Despite what can only be described as incredibly heroic efforts, they were unable to do so, and President Reagan was pronounced dead, having never regained consciousness.

"Of the two bullet wounds, the head wound was clearly the more serious, and has preliminarily been determined to be the cause of death. That tentative conclusion is, of course, subject to the results of a full autopsy which will be conducted later this morning. Based on the initial pathology reports, it appears that bullet entered the President's skull about 3 centimeters above the top of his left ear on a slightly upward angle. Given the scope and magnitude of the damage that was observed, it seems apparent that the bullet exploded upon entering the brain. The law enforcement authorities have told us that the bullet that struck the President's head is called a 'Devastator' and is designed to do exactly what it did.

"When this bullet explosively fragmented, it caused massive and irreparable trauma to the left cerebrum and to a significant portion of the stem, which is the part of the brain which controls respiration and other autonomic functions.

"For the record, the other bullet entered the President's body on the left side of his torso just under his armpit. That bullet broke a rib and lodged in his left lung very close to his heart. This second bullet did not explode, and has in fact been extracted. The shape of that extracted slug, flattened like a small coin, suggests that it probably ricocheted off a hard surface before entering the President's torso.

"In anticipation of your questions, although the body wound was serious and was potentially life-threatening, no medical conclusions have yet been drawn concerning whether President Reagan might have survived had the torso injury been his only wound.

"At any rate, the head wound made any such question moot. I'll now take a few questions."

CHAPTER 3

Elmendorf Air Force Base
Anchorage, Alaska
0830 hours, 31 March 1981

It seemed so bizarrely surreal, Captain Jackson Felix Kuhn – "Jack" to his friends – thought to himself, mentally recounting the events of the last 24 hours. Yesterday at this time, he'd just walked into the military courtroom at the far end of the legal office on the second floor of the group headquarters building to prosecute what promised to be a "cakewalk" special court-martial.

The trial participants – including the young two-striper who had decided to take a vacation without benefit of commander approval and hocked his roommate's expensive watch to help finance it – fidgeted at their assigned places, waiting for the judge to enter and begin the proceedings. They had been surprised when the judge entered the courtroom sans black robe, looking like the lieutenant colonel he was when not cloaked in his judicial outer garment. The judge had walked to the middle of the courtroom instead of to his bench.

"People," the California-based judge had said somberly, "we're going to delay this trial until tomorrow. I just heard on the radio coming over here that President Reagan has been shot. Return to your duties, and plan on reconvening tomorrow at oh nine hundred unless you hear differently from me before then."

After turning the young accused back over to the custody of his first sergeant, Kuhn and Captain Larry Wilkins, the defense counsel in the case, had hurried down the hallway from the courtroom straight to the base staff judge advocate's office. They hoped and suspected his TV might be on.

It was.

Lieutenant Colonel John Scott, the base Staff Judge Advocate (SJA) – militaryspeak for an organization's senior lawyer – and three other young officers assigned to the legal office were all soberly focused on the 12" black and white television Scott kept in his office, mostly so he could watch NFL football on the Sunday mornings he routinely spent in the office catching up on paperwork from the past week.

Noticing Kuhn and Wilkins at his open doorway, he had motioned them to come in and sit down.

"What's happening, sir?" asked Kuhn.

"Not really sure," Scott had replied. "All they're saying is that the President's been shot and taken to the hospital."

After a few minutes of silently staring at the little TV, it was obvious that was just about all the media knew for the moment – that Reagan and several other people had been injured, that they'd apparently been shot by a "lone gunman" (wasn't it always a lone gunman?) who was now in custody, and that the President was undergoing emergency surgery at the George Washington University Medical Center.

"Okay guys, get back to work for now," said Scott a few more minutes later, after it was clear that it would likely be a while before anything further was known. He had promised to call everybody back in when there were new developments.

Both the prosecutor and defense counsel then moved down the hall to Kuhn's own office, significantly smaller and clearly less well furnished than the SJA's.

Because Wilkins' area defense counsel office was two blocks away, and since he had no client appointments scheduled (he'd thought he'd be in court all day), the defense lawyer decided he'd just as well hang around Kuhn's office for a while. There was no TV, but Kuhn switched on his portable radio to monitor events, turning the volume down to just audible.

Kuhn and Wilkins had already become pretty good friends during this tour, at least when they weren't slugging it out in the courtroom. Jack had discovered that they had a lot in common. For starters, both JAGs had Big Ten roots – Kuhn's bachelor's degree was from the University of Illinois and his juris doctorate from Northwestern, and although Wilkins had attended the Air Force Academy as an undergrad, he had earned his law degree from Indiana University under the Air Force's funded legal education program (FLEP). Both were competent athletes who still enjoyed playing pickup basketball at the base gym at lunchtime and slow-pitch softball during the summer in the Anchorage city league, and both were married to girls from their Midwest hometowns.

There were differences, of course – Kuhn had two young daughters, while Wilkins and his wife had yet to start a family. Kuhn suspected that might have a lot to do with Wilkins' extraordinary ambition – Larry probably figured that kids would be too much of a distraction and counterproductive to his career goals. Wilkins made no secret of his desire to get ahead. He'd once mentioned to Kuhn, almost in passing, that he was certain he would eventually get promoted to general and would likely be the Air Force Judge Advocate General, known universally among military members as "TJAG," someday. That assertion had struck Jack as more than a little presumptuous at this very early point in Wilkins' military career, particularly since there were over twelve hundred JAGs in the Air Force and only four of them were general officers. He remembered thinking at the time that the Academy's reputation for producing Air Force officers with massive egos was probably well-deserved. Larry's boundless ambition and apparent self-confidence notwithstanding, Jack still considered him a good guy and a loyal friend.

"Do you remember where you were when Kennedy got shot?" Wilkins asked.

"Sure I do. I was in Mr. Bannister's freshman biology class in high school. He was diagramming a frog's heart on the blackboard – I can still see it in my mind's eye – when the principal came over the loudspeaker to say that Kennedy had been shot. A few minutes later, he came back on to say that he was dead. How about you?"

"Pretty much the same," replied Wilkins, "I was in gym class and we were running laps around the basketball court when I heard."

"Wonder how bad Reagan's really hurt?" the defense counsel then asked.

"No way of knowing for sure, of course, but my guess is that they'd have already said something if he wasn't hurt pretty bad," opined the prosecutor.

"You might be right," agreed Wilkins. "It's spooky about the twenty-year curse," he continued, referring to the well-known historical happenstance that every president elected in twenty-year intervals since Lincoln had died in office.

"We probably ought not bury him yet," answered Kuhn, "but you're right, it's spooky."

"What do you know about Bush?" Wilkins asked his friend.

"Damn little, except that he's from Texas, he used to run the CIA, and he comes from money I think," was Jack's answer.

Sometime later, Scott's secretary had come to Jack's office door to beckon them back to the SJA's office. When Kuhn and Wilkins got there a few seconds later, it was standing room only. It seemed to Kuhn like every one of the 18 folks assigned to the legal office – officers, civilians, and NCOs – were now crowded in Scott's office all staring at the little TV on top of his bookcase.

"They're saying the White House is going to make an announcement," said Scott quietly to his newest arrivals.

Captain Kuhn glanced at the clock on the wall. Almost 11 a.m. here in Alaska, he noted, 5 p.m. on the East Coast.

The NBC affiliate they were watching had then cut to a feed of Alexander Haig, the Secretary of State for the new Administration. He was flanked by what looked like James Baker, Reagan's chief of staff, and another man Kuhn didn't recognize. They appeared to be somewhere in the White House, but Kuhn couldn't tell exactly where. There also appeared to be at least a couple dozen other folks, reporters he assumed, to whom Haig spoke.

"It is my sad duty to report that President Reagan died about 40 minutes ago as a result of the wounds he received earlier today outside the Hilton Hotel. The Vice President is in the air at this moment on his way back to Washington. As Secretary of State, I'm in control here at the White House pending the Vice President's return. More information will be provided you later this evening."

Haig is still a commander at heart, Kuhn mused to himself as he watched the retired Army four-star stepping up to take charge in a crisis. He wondered, however, if Bush and his people would much appreciate the "in control at the White House" comment or the fact that he still referred to the new President by his old title.

It seemed to those watching that the cadre of reporters all shouted as one, their fusillade of simultaneous questions creating an unintelligible din. Neither Haig nor the other two men paused to acknowledge the interrogatories, instead turning quickly away from the cameras and departing the room. The little TV screen returned to a picture of John Chancellor in the NBC studio.

"Crap, not again," muttered Scott; many others in the small office gasped out similar reflexive epithets. Almost immediately, though, Scott resumed his normal unemotional and businesslike demeanor. "Gang, it's likely we'll be going to a higher alert posture for at least a day or two while the folks at the Pentagon make sure there's no more to this than meets the eye. Make sure you all let the on-call JAG know where you can be reached after duty-hours in case we have a recall."

With that, Lieutenant Colonel Scott strode purposefully out of his crowded office to head downstairs to the command section, where he correctly anticipated that the commander would soon be convening the wing battle staff to review events and assess the situation.

Their boss now departed, most everyone else had then wandered quietly back to their own desks, though a few remained behind in Scott's office to keep watching the little TV for a while longer.

The rest of yesterday afternoon at work had been almost totally non-productive for Kuhn, at least in terms of doing the many legal tasks the Air Force paid him to do. Rather, he had spent a lot of the afternoon staring out his office window at the Chugach Foothills in the distance, reflecting on what had just happened. Even though it was almost April, the foothills were still covered, in fact all of Anchorage was still covered, with a ubiquitous blanket of snow that had been in place since late September. In a couple of weeks, Kuhn knew, that blanket would morph into a treacherous mass of icy gray muddy mush during what Alaskans understatedly called "breakup."

Staring idly at the currently serene Alaskan landscape, Kuhn had thought that this felt much different from when JFK had been murdered. Reagan's death didn't seem to engender the same kind of stunned horror, unbelievable shock, and "all is lost" despair he remembered feeling on that cold November day almost eighteen years ago.

Maybe it was because he was so much younger and more impressionable then, he thought. Maybe, too, it was because he and everybody else in the country had by now been calloused and their nerve-endings deadened by a seemingly unending string of American assassinations and assassination attempts in the years since. Martin Luther King and Bobby Kennedy, of course, but also the two unsuccessful attempts on President Ford, and Arthur Bremer's very nearly successful effort that left George Wallace crippled for life.

No, Kuhn felt like a rug had been pulled out from under him. The past few months had seen an extraordinary period of growing "feel-good" optimism and increasing confidence unlike anything he could remember.

There'd been several harbingers of better things to come. Reagan's huge landslide win in November over Carter, whom Jack considered an embarrassingly inept president. The American hockey team's unbelievably uplifting upset win over the vaunted Soviets in the Lake Placid Olympics – the Wing Commander had even allowed the score to be painted on the left side of the four F-4 jets sitting alert at King Salmon, so that it would be clearly visible to the crew of the next Russian bear bomber the jets encountered during the routine intercepts that occurred between Alaska and Siberia. The inspiring inauguration speech of a strong new president who promised better times ahead for the country and looked like he could carry through on that promise. And the almost immediate release of the long-held American hostages in Tehran by the Islamic Republic of Iran, whose leaders apparently concluded it best not to test the mettle or resolve of the new President.

And not coincidentally, Kuhn and most of the officers he knew had also developed a new spring in their collective step at the prospect of serving a Commander-in Chief who appreciated the military, and understood how badly those in uniform had been treated in recent years.

It wasn't just things like the promised "catch-up" pay raise (which he and Margie would certainly appreciate, of course), but rather the prospect of being in on the ground floor for the American military renaissance that Reagan had promised. In Kuhn's case, that meant to finally be part of an Air Force that would at long last be funded, manned, armed, and trained to be the very best in the world.

He wondered if George Bush – make that President Bush, he corrected himself – shared Reagan's strong and hopeful vision. And assuming he did, whether he possessed the necessary political clout and charisma to turn that vision into reality. Jack didn't know the answer to either question.

Jack's train of thought was suddenly broken when the bailiff knocked on his office door to remind him that the one day-delayed court-martial would convene in ten minutes. Kuhn put his wondering on hold and headed back to the courtroom. The military judge would be wearing his robe today – it was time to go back to work.

CHAPTER 4

The White House, Washington, D.C.
9:00 a.m., October 15, 1983

It was a small but exceedingly powerful group that had assembled this Saturday morning in the Oval Office. In addition to the President, Secretary of State George Schultz was there, along with Secretary of Defense Dick Cheney, Chairman of the Joint Chiefs of Staff John Vessey, and CIA Director Bill Casey.

The subject was Grenada.

Schultz was doing the talking. "As you know, Mr. President, Grenada is a small Caribbean island about 100 miles north of Venezuela. The country has cozied up to the Cubans ever since Maurice Bishop came to power in 1979. Bishop was an avowed Marxist, and our friend Fidel helped prop him up with money and arms for the past four years. He's even sent some soldiers and construction workers to help build Grenada a new airport, which obviously will give Castro access to a very convenient location for any South American adventures he might have in mind."

Casey nodded assent.

"Apparently, however," Schultz continued, "Bishop wasn't communist enough to suit his Deputy PM, a guy named Coard. Day before yesterday, Coard pulled off a pretty bloody coup, killing Bishop in the process."

"Do we think the Cubans are behind the coup?" President Bush asked, turning to Casey.

"No way of knowing for sure yet, Mr. President," answered the CIA Director, "but I don't think so."

"Okay," said Bush, "continue George."

"The situation there is still somewhat unstable, but it looks like the new government should be able to consolidate their position pretty quickly. And there seems little doubt that it will be even less friendly to us than Bishop's was."

"What are our options?" asked the President.

"Well, we can pursue this thing diplomatically," answered SecState, "with a standard shot across the bow condemning the violence and warning Coard about the potential consequences if any Americans there are harmed."

"How many Americans are there on Grenada?" asked Bush.

"Turns out there are almost a thousand Americans living on the island," answered Schultz.

"No kidding," the President responded, "that's a lot higher than I would have thought. What are they all doing there?"

"Most are students at a private medical school there, mostly well-off kids who couldn't get into any American medical school," Schultz replied.

"I'll be damned," said the President. "Are they in any danger?"

Casey responded to that one. "Probably no more than anyone else on the island. But there are a lot of crazies with guns down there right now, and probably will be until this thing settles down. My analysts think, though, that Coard is smart enough to know that hurting one of our people would give us a legitimate reason to enter the fray."

"OK, let's talk about military options" Bush said, turning to Cheney and Vessey.

Cheney responded. "If you're asking whether we could go in there and take out Coard, the answer is yes. General Vessey estimates that we could probably get the job done with a force of less than 10,000. Our Rapid Deployment Force is built for this kind of thing."

"What parts of the RDF would you deploy to do this job, John?" asked the President of Vessey.

"In terms of boots on the ground, I think all it would take would be a couple Ranger battalions, some paratroopers from the 82nd Airborne at Fort Bragg, along with a few Marine units and some Delta Force and SEAL special operators." said Vessey.

"Any estimate of likely casualties we should anticipate if we go in there?" asked President Bush.

"Anytime we go in shooting, you'd have to expect some losses," the Army four-star answered. "But they'd likely not be huge numbers – I'd be surprised if we lost any more than a few dozen KIA."

The president turned back to Cheney. "How many Cubans soldiers do we think Castro has on the island, Dick?"

"We believe the number to be around 500, although it's sometimes difficult to distinguish the Cuban military folks from the civilians, primarily engineers and construction workers, Fidel's sent there." SecDef responded.

"Would they fight if we decided to go in?" asked Bush.

"We have to assume they would," Cheney answered honestly.

"By the way, Mr. President, there are also about fifty Russians on the island," interjected Casey, "not to mention a few dozen East Germans, Libyans and North Koreans. We don't think they're military types, but some are clearly spooks who know how to fire a weapon."

"So, if we try to invade," the President continued, "we'll likely be in the position of having to kill some Cubans in the process, not to mention risk killing some stray Russians who might happen to get in the way of our bullets."

"Probably right," admitted the Secretary of Defense.

"O.K., I get the picture," said the President. "Assuming we want to go in, how would we justify it politically?"

Schultz answered that one. "Some of my folks think we could hang our hat on rescuing the American students there."

"But you said you don't think they're in any kind of imminent danger," responded the President.

"Nevertheless, the situation there is extremely volatile," answered SecState. "Who's to say that one of the factions or even the new government might decide to increase their leverage by kidnapping some of them, like Hezbollah has done in Lebanon or the Iranians did after the Shah fell."

"That's a pretty long stretch," answered a clearly skeptical Bush. "I'm not sure that dog will hunt. Any chance the U.N. or the Organization of American States would support military action?"

"Realistically, sir, no," admitted Schultz, "but there may be another organization that would be willing to endorse a military move against Coard. The Organization of Eastern Caribbean States is made up of nine small island states on that side of the Caribbean, including Grenada – most of them are plenty nervous about what's going on and worry whether they might be next on Castro's list. It's likely that the eight countries in that organization other than Grenada could be enticed to come on board and support military operations."

"Jesus, I'm not sure anybody's ever even heard of that organization," responded the President. "Let me see if I understand what you're telling me. A Marxist dictator on a piss-ant little island just got overthrown and blown away by another Marxist dictator. And if we decide we want to take out the new guy, we'd have to justify it on the grounds of rescuing American medical students who may well not really be in much jeopardy, sacrifice the lives of some number of young American GIs, kill some Cubans and maybe some Russians along the way and piss off most of the rest of the world in the process, and give an already hostile Congress even more ammunition to use against this Administration. Do I have it about right?"

No one answered him. The Oval Office visitors remained silent while the President pondered the equities for several long seconds. George Bush knew better than most that war – even a small war in which victory was certain – was not a venture to be undertaken lightly. As a naval aviator in World War II, he'd experienced the terrible reality of combat at age 19. Too many of his friends and comrades had had to pay the ultimate price that war invariably exacts. Hell, he himself had come far too close to paying that price when his torpedo bomber had been shot up and he'd had to ditch in the Pacific. World War II was a war, Bush knew, that had to be fought. An invasion of Grenada, he decided, did not.

After a minute or so, the President spoke. "Bill," he said looking at Casey, "for right now, Grenada is matter for the CIA, and not DoD. Keep me posted on any new developments, and come back and see me in a week or so about possible covert options."

President Bush turned to Cheney and Vessey. "Dick, General, have your folks work up some contingency plans for military operations just in case we need them, but keep them compartmentalized and really close hold."

"Any questions?" asked the President of the United States.

There were none.

CHAPTER 5

Maxwell Air Force Base
Montgomery, Alabama
1030 hours, 4 December 1984

It was a perfect nickname for this huge auditorium, Jack Kuhn thought – the "Big Blue Bedroom."

As he sat in his assigned seat in the fifteenth row of the large Air Command and Staff College lecture hall, Kuhn didn't have to look hard to find evidence supporting the aptness of the hall's unofficial moniker – the Army officer directly in front of him was slumped low in his theatre style chair, the top of his balding head barely protruding above the seat back. And although Jack couldn't see his face, he'd bet a case of beer that the ground-pounder's eyes were comfortably closed.

Jack decided he ought not be too judgmental, realizing that he himself was only paying intermittently scant attention to the speaker on the stage, a bearded Ph.D. from the State Department who was droning on about what he believed was an impending economic and political crisis facing the Soviet Union, and how that "crisis" presented the ideal opportunity for the U.S. military to at long last dramatically draw down its overall force structure and its overly robust and expensive presence throughout Europe.

Despite having to endure an occasional boring (and simplistically illogical, at least to Jack's way of thinking) speaker like the current egghead, Major Jack Kuhn knew that getting selected to attend ACSC had been a real break for his career. Only five JAGs were chosen each year to attend the prestigious mid-career course reserved for the Air Force's fast burners. There were around five hundred folks attending the ten-month course, about 75% of them USAF majors like Jack.

The rest of the class roster was filled out by about sixty field grade officers from the other services, as well as another seventy-five or so "international officers" from around the world.

Those foreign officers ran the full gamut, Jack had observed, from the hard-working and stoic Koreans to the hard-partying and extraordinarily affable Canucks and Aussies. There were also a number of representatives from central and South America, several from Europe, and a couple dozen attendees from the Middle East, including three very serious Israeli officers.

Kuhn had noticed, without any real surprise, that the Israelis didn't interact much with their Arab counterparts, particularly the Saudis. For their part, the Saudis didn't seem much interested in interacting with *any* of their non-Saudi classmates – it was a class joke that the Kingdom's contingent wasn't overly concerned with academic achievement, or even with regular attendance. Although cutting class was not, of course, a viable option for any of the American officers attending ACSC, that rule didn't seem to be strictly applied to some of the foreign attendees.

The student grapevine had even reported that a couple of the Saudi officers were "royals" – among the over 20,000 descendants of Abdul Aziz, the founder and first king of Saudi Arabia – and that their "student housing" consisted of a lavishly upscale private mansion somewhere on the east side of Montgomery. The rumor mill also buzzed that the mansion was the site for frequent all night parties hosted by its rich occupants, which Jack thought might well account for their rather casual adherence to the "requirement" of classroom attendance.

Different strokes for different folks, he thought.

He, Margie, and the girls were also living on the east side of town, though certainly not in a mansion. Theirs was, however, a terrific house for the four of them, a four-bedroom brick ranch in a nice neighborhood that came with a wonderful "extra," an in-ground swimming pool in the back yard. The rent he paid – it was owned by an Air War College colonel who had been reassigned out of the area – was a smidge less than $600 a month, a figure their budget could tolerate.

Although the house was great, and God knows the girls were getting full use out of the pool, there was an additional major expense that came with living in Montgomery. He and Margie had decided to dip into their none-too-robust savings account to let Heather and Cindy, now 10 and 8, attend fourth and second grades, respectively, at St. James Academy. The private school had been in their view the only responsible alternative to what passed for public education in Alabama, a far cry from the terrific public elementary schools they had enjoyed in Alaska.

Despite the extra expense, ACSC had thus far been a glorious year. Kuhn immensely enjoyed many of the fellow students he had met and gotten to know, and was, he thought, gaining a great deal of big-picture insight from the exceptionally good (mostly) speakers – the bore still talking on stage notwithstanding – who came here to lecture.

He was also enjoying the respite of the short sabbatical from the day-to-day practice of military law, and the unusual freedom that had come with not being responsible, at least for a little while, for anyone other than himself. Although, at least for the American students, there was plenty of reading to keep up with and a thesis that would be due in the spring, he was able to spend more quality time with his family than at any time since he and Margie had gotten married in 1972 while he was still a law student.

Margie seemed to be enjoying the year as well. They'd decided it didn't make much sense for her to try to substitute teach during their short stay in Alabama, a decision made easier by the miserly pittance that Montgomery schools paid their subs. She had made friends with a few of the other wives of his section mates, attended most of the various social functions put on by ACSC, and even had brought the girls out a couple of times to see Section 34 play softball. *I still can play a pretty decent shortstop*, Jack thought immodestly.

It was hard to believe they'd already been married for almost twelve years. He supposed that most couples married that long experienced a similar reduction in passion such as had occurred between Margie and him over the past few years. Part of it, he knew, was his own damn fault. His obsessive preoccupation with his legal duties had translated into an awful lot of extra hours at the office during his last assignment – *the law is a jealous mistress*, he remembered reading somewhere during his first year of law school. He had secretly hoped that a less stressful year of scholarly academic pursuits might help jumpstart Margie's interest in participating in a somewhat more active love life, but that had not yet been the case.

But Margie was a loyal wife, Jack knew, and a good mother to their two daughters. And it wasn't like they never did it – they just didn't do it as much as Jack would like.

After graduation from the U of I, he'd gone back home to Lake Forest for the summer, and re-met Margie Donnelly – whom he hadn't seen since high school – one evening in June at Bill's Pizza Pub in nearby Mundelein. They had their first date the following weekend, and by the end of the summer were seeing each other frequently and exclusively – Margie was very good-looking and very smart, and they'd had a wonderful summer courting each other.

After they'd gone back to school – he to Northwestern for his first year of law school and she to Purdue for her senior year as an education major, he'd made the two-and-a-half-hour drive from Evanston to Lafayette at least once a month to see her. They'd gotten married the following summer right after she graduated, and Heather had come along less than a year later. After he got his law degree, the three of them had headed off to his first assignment at Pease Air Force Base in New Hampshire – Cindy had been born in the base hospital there.

Kuhn was interrupted from his mental walk down memory lane by the sound of subdued laughter. Was it possible this speaker had actually tried to make a joke? If so, Jack hadn't heard it. He looked up at the egghead in time to see him smile briefly before continuing his painfully dull monologue.

Kuhn looked down at his watch. *Christ, this guy's not even halfway through*, he silently lamented. As best Jack could tell, the speaker hadn't said anything in the first thirty minutes of the lecture that deviated from his twenty-page article that Jack and his classmates had been assigned to read in preparation for this lecture. Jack tuned him out again.

Remembering he needed to schedule an oil change for the car before heading up to Illinois for the holidays, he made his first notation of the day in the open notebook on his lap.

Jack wasn't especially looking forward to the upcoming Christmas trip – there'd be a lot of driving, and the weather up north this time of year was chancy at best. They planned to spend a couple days with Margie's folks at their new place just outside of St. Louis – Mr. Donnelly had taken a management job with Boeing there about a year ago – and then head up north of Chicago to see his mom.

That was going to be the tough part, Jack predicted to himself. Even though his folks had divorced several years ago, this would be Mom's first Christmas since Dad passed away – Felix Kuhn had died at age 60 of a massive heart attack eight months ago.

Unlike Dad, who had married his thirty-something legal secretary mere weeks after the divorce was final, Mom had never remarried. Thank God, Jack thought, Mom had gotten the house and her attorney had negotiated a provision requiring Dad to keep her as the beneficiary of a $200,000 life insurance policy. Despite Dad's obvious (at least in retrospect) philandering and the fact that most of his financial estate had been conveyed to his new young widow, Jack knew that his mom still regarded her late ex-husband with some considerable ambivalence, and that the holidays would be tough for her this year.

Hell, thought Jack, *he* regarded his dad with ambivalence. Even though he loathed the fact that his father's loose zipper had caused Mom so much pain, his dad had nevertheless been an enormous influence on him. A second-generation attorney, Felix Kuhn had in many ways been Jack's professional role model. He had also, not insignificantly, borne most of the economic burden of putting Jack through college and law school.

The elder Kuhn had been supportive of Jack's decision to join the Air Force ROTC program during his freshman year at Illinois back in 1967. With no end in sight to the Vietnam quagmire, they had both agreed that becoming an Air Force officer was a much preferable alternative to being drafted into the Army as an enlisted grunt. And Dad had been very pleased when the Air Force had granted Jack a three-year "educational delay" after college in order to attend law school. The elder Kuhn had told him that spending four years as a judge advocate wouldn't be a bad way to begin his legal career.

Jack's decision to stay beyond that initial four-year commitment had, on the other hand, not pleased his father at all, who derided his decision as foolish and "waste of his education and talents." Those talents could better and much more profitably be applied in the civilian world, the senior Kuhn had vociferously argued to his only son. His dad had even offered Jack a position in his own Chicago law firm, along with an implicit promise of early partner status.

Jack, of course, knew a lot more than his father about what it meant to be a judge advocate. He had believed then (and still believed now) that the legal challenges he got to deal with, the large measure of responsibility he got to shoulder, and the intangible rewards – particularly in terms of personal satisfaction – of being a JAG were much more important to him than chasing the bucks as a civilian personal injury practitioner. So, contrary to his father's strong wishes and unequivocal guidance, Jack had not put in a request for separation when his commitment was up in 1978, instead accepting reassignment to Alaska.

His father had died, Jack knew, still thinking his son naïve and ungrateful. Jack also knew that he would always regret his failure to make his dad understand his decision to make the military his career. *Nothing to be done about it now*, Jack thought.

Polite but subdued applause in the auditorium signaled the unexpected end (at least to Jack and likely to the sleeping Army officer in front of him) of the lecture, and immediately brought Major Kuhn back to the here and now. He closed his notebook with its one entry about the oil change and headed out of the lecture hall toward the seminar room where he and his 11 fellow section members would spend the last hour of this morning and all afternoon preparing for next week's computerized war game against another section.

That promised to be a lot more interesting than the lecture he had just not listened to.

A few minutes later, he and his section mates were sitting in the small classroom that was home to Section 34 waiting for Lt Col Stenborg, their assigned faculty advisor, to arrive to lead the preparations. It was past 1100 hours, and Stenborg had still not arrived. Suddenly, a full colonel walked unannounced into the room, and all twelve members of the Section instinctively and immediately got to their feet. "Sit down, gang," said Colonel Watson, Deputy Commandant of ACSC. "Colonel Stenborg won't be here today . . . he was in a fender bender this morning downtown on the way to base and got banged up a little – I'm hearing his left arm is broken. He's at the base hospital right now getting patched up and is going to be fine, but we're going to have to postpone your section's war game preparation sessions until he returns later this week. That means you all are on your own time until tomorrow morning."

Less than an hour later, Jack was driving his three-year-old Mustang across town heading for home. He thought he'd surprise Margie and take her to lunch, something they got to do too rarely given his own busy schedule and the obvious non-stop demands of raising their two high maintenance young daughters . . . *aren't all kids high maintenance*, Jack thought. But since the girls were in school right now, this seemed like a perfect chance to be an attentive husband for at least a little while.

He decided to take the northern bypass around downtown to avoid the construction on I-85, the area where his faculty advisor's accident had occurred. As Jack passed Emory Road, he noticed the green sign for Gunter Air Force Station, a smaller systems command base also in Montgomery where his good friend Larry Wilkins was now stationed as the deputy staff judge advocate. He thought momentarily about stopping by the legal office there to see how Larry was doing, but almost immediately decided instead to stick to Plan A and take Margie to lunch. He saw Larry relatively frequently, most recently at happy hour at the Gunter Officers Club last Friday. Larry was always a fun guy to hang around with, the ultimate "hail fellow well met" people person in almost every social setting. He was also Jack's closest confidant among all the folks he had met during his years in the Air Force. When Jack concluded he'd had a little too much beer at happy hour last week, it had been Larry who'd shuttled him home in his brand-new silver 280Z. Jack smiled as he remembered the standing joke that Air Force Academy grads were all hard-wired to buy hot sports cars . . . Larry was no exception to that apparent truism. Although the alcohol-induced fog of that evening dulled his memory of the ride a bit, Jack seemed to recall sharing some of his marital frustrations with Larry during that the trip home. He was lucky, he knew, to have a friend like him with whom he could share virtually anything.

Jack's thoughts turned back to Margie. It was just a little after noon, and he decided he'd take her to that new Italian place on the eastern bypass for her surprise luncheon date. He smiled at the thought of how pleased she'd be.

Fifteen minutes later he was almost home. As he turned onto his street, he was surprised to see a silver 280Z parked in front of his house.

CHAPTER 6

The White House, Washington, D.C.
6:30 a.m., January 20, 1985

President George Herbert Walker Bush sat alone in the Oval Office. Given that it was the last morning he'd ever spend in the office (at least while it was *his* office), he had arrived somewhat earlier than was his normal practice.

There wasn't a lot to do. He had signed the obligatory last minute Presidential pardons (not very many, really) the night before, and been thoroughly briefed on the choreography of the inaugural ceremony which would take place in just a few hours. As the outgoing President, he didn't have a large or very meaningful part in the ceremony . . . mostly his job was to try to look "Presidential" and magnanimous while watching Walter Mondale take the oath of office as the 42nd President of the United States.

As he reclined in his desk chair and uncharacteristically put his feet up on the absolutely empty desktop, he mused to himself that in some ways he had been very much looking forward to this day. Truth be known, he thought, he was damn glad that his three year, nine month, three week Presidency was now almost over – it had been no fun at all.

The cards had, he knew, been badly stacked against him from the start, particularly since the circumstances of his ascension did not include the political mandate that comes with having been elected to this office. Further, he had never been particularly close to President Reagan or his inner circle, due in no small part to their frequently acrimonious primary battle in 1980, which had made for an extremely uncomfortable transition. Most of Reagan's key staff had, in fact, packed up and left town within three months of their president's death, leaving Bush with the impossible task of trying to put together an effective team of his own on the fly.

And although he obviously could never say so publicly, Bush knew with certainty that the two promises which got Reagan elected in his 1980 landslide win over Jimmy Carter . . . reviving the economy with massive tax cuts while at the same time increasing military spending to unprecedented peacetime levels . . . were fool's gold of the worst kind. Unfortunately for him, Bush thought bitterly, it was he, and not the dead president, who took the fall for failure to fulfill Reagan's impossible political promises to the American people.

In that sense, the former president had been lucky to die when he did, Bush morbidly mused. . . by being assassinated just two months into his term, Reagan never had to suffer the inevitable consequences of voodoo economic fixes and over-the-top defense proposals which no Congress would or could ever support.

Congress, he frowned as he thought. *Has any President ever been dealt a worse hand?* He rhetorically wondered. His "honeymoon" with lawmakers after succeeding the murdered Reagan had been so short as to never have occurred.

What really irked him were those Republicans, relatively few in number but huge in terms of the final outcome, who had disloyally jumped ship and failed to support the Administration in the summer of '81 when the Reagan tax cut plan and defense budgets, which Bush had inherited, were narrowly but convincingly defeated on Capitol Hill. Everything had gone downhill from that point on.

After the 1982 Congressional election debacle, of course, in which the Democrats won a staggering 63% of House seats and achieved a 61-39 majority in the Senate, he had been doomed to spend his last two years in office as the lamest of presidential ducks since Andrew Johnson.

He had been frustrated beyond words when many in his own party had impaled him for attempting to find some areas of cooperation and accommodation with the overwhelmingly Democratic Congress, most especially the 1983 income tax increase compromise he had reluctantly agreed to. If he had vetoed the bill as many in his party had urged him to do, Congress would have easily overridden and he would have looked even more impotent. Better to be perceived as a pragmatic statesman than a political eunuch, he remembered thinking at the time.

His cooperation with the Congress on raising taxes had probably been, he now realized, a major political miscalculation on his part. Not only had his stance alienated so many voters from his own party, but it had also had the unintended effect of taking Mondale (whose well-known support for higher taxes would likely have been a huge campaign liability had not Bush already inadvertently done his dirty work for him) off the hook with the electorate.

There had been many other distractions, of course, particularly in the foreign policy arena.

The terrible suicide bombing of the Marine barracks in Lebanon fifteen months earlier had clearly been the low point. Bush had ordered the peace-keeping role for the Marines, over the initial objection of some of his senior generals in the Pentagon, in the hope of helping extract America's staunch ally Israel from the horrible mess they had gotten into when they invaded Lebanon. Bush knew at the time it was a high-risk gambit, but thought the chance worth taking, particularly if America could come out of the mission viewed as an "honest broker" by both sides to the Middle East conflict. It had never occurred to him (or apparently to any of the State Department planners who had put together the concept and sold it him) that so many Americans could be killed in a single terrorist attack. After that debacle, and the inevitable Monday morning criticism that he had been reckless with the lives of hundreds of young American Marines, caution had to henceforth be the watchword for his Administration when it came to the use of military force in pursuit of American foreign policy objectives.

His best and most important foreign policy decision, in fact, had been one of prudence and caution. As cruel fate would have it, however, that decision – to significantly ratchet down the United States' covert involvement in the Afghanistan mess – was literally invisible to the American public, hidden behind the highest of code-word security classifications. The CIA (and Bush knew well from his short tenure as its head that agency's bent for high-risk adventurism) had wanted to funnel huge additional amounts of money and modern arms to the Mujahadeen rebels in Afghanistan battling the Soviet occupiers who continued to prop up – at considerable human cost – the puppet government in Kabul they had installed in 1979. From all the President could tell, the Soviet Union was already thoroughly stuck on the Afghanistan flypaper without any help from the U.S. At the end of the day, however, Bush knew that no matter how well armed the Muslim rebels might become, they really had no chance of ultimate victory against the determined Soviet military juggernaut.

He'd be damned if he'd pour precious dollars down that black hole and leave American fingerprints all over the rebels' lost cause. Of course, he'd never get any public credit for that bit of wisdom.

No . . . what the public would remember was Lebanon and goddamn Grenada, a piss-ant country of no importance to anyone other than the political crucifiers in this country. The overly sensationalized Cuban defense cooperation treaty with Grenada meant virtually nothing from a geopolitical standpoint, he knew. It certainly didn't constitute the kind of "clear and present" threat to national security that would prompt any rational president to opt for military action. Even if he had wanted to "send in the Marines," of course, he knew that neither Congress nor public opinion still scarred by the Vietnam experience would support shedding one drop of American blood over a meaningless tiny Caribbean island. Yet many in his own party, and even some among the Democrats, had the temerity to distort his prudence and argue that failure to intervene in Grenada meant he was a "wimp" when it came to foreign policy. Many of them, of course, were the same SOBs who had criticized him for being too reckless in Lebanon.

And then there was young George W., whose purported – and widely reported – indiscretions of a few years back hadn't helped Bush's political standing either. Hell, the elder Bush thought, he'd caroused some and probably driven drunk himself at some point when he was young and stupid. Of course, he hadn't been a president's son and the carnivorous press hadn't circled over him like the sleazy vultures they were when he was a thirty-something.

President Bush had once hoped that his eldest son, with his good looks, "aw-shucks" charm, Texas common sense and Ivy League education, would someday be a credible candidate for high office. He would have been terrific, his father thought, in the Texas state legislature, as Governor of the Lone Star State, or maybe even in this town. Such a future was, unfortunately, highly unlikely now given the profoundly unfair but thorough painting he had received from the media as the irresponsibly "wild and crazy" son of a President. It was the kind of character issue that he was afraid would dog his son for the rest of his life. No, it wasn't fair at all, but Bush knew from painful personal experience that little in life was.

At least now, Bush thought with just a small bit of satisfaction, Johnny Carson will have to find somebody other than his oldest son to serve as nightly fodder for his lowbrow monologue.

Thank God Jeb has stayed under the radar, he told himself, thanks in large part he knew to George W.'s involuntary monopoly on the tabloid headlines over the past few years. *Maybe Jeb will be able to carry the family political torch when he gets older*, the outgoing President thought hopefully.

The soon to be ex-president turned his gaze out the window toward the Washington monument and noticed the dawn sky was beginning to brighten. Yep, Bush concluded to himself, *all in all it's been a pretty crappy four years.*

The only good news, he reminded himself, was that it was Bob Dole who, after committing the politically fratricidal (and, as it turned out, politically *suicidal*) act of successfully challenging an incumbent President from his own party for the 1984 Republican nomination, had paid the piper bigtime.

Dole had won only two states – Kansas and Wyoming with their combined 10 electoral votes – and less than 38% of the national popular vote in November. Bush guessed that Barry Goldwater must be delighted to the point of ecstasy to have finally relinquished his title as the biggest Republican presidential loser of modern times.

There was one other piece of good news, he remembered. It would now be that socialist Fritz Mondale, his lightweight young Veep Al Gore, and the still massively Democratic Congress who would be blamed if the American economy continued to languish, as seemed likely.

The best news of all, he smiled as he thought, was that he'd be in Kennebunkport by dinnertime. *I'm not going to miss this shithole one goddamn bit!*

CHAPTER 7

Wurtsmith Air Force Base
Oscoda, Michigan
0600 hours, 23 February 1985

You'd think those three years in Alaska would have earned me a warm weather assignment, Major Jack Kuhn thought ruefully as he quickly stepped out the front door of his three-bedroom base house on Nebraska Street. Not exactly stylishly clad in blue jeans, red bathrobe, and tan slippers, he rushed down the steps to retrieve the Saturday edition of the Detroit *Free Press* that unfortunately lay just out of easy reach in the snowbank next to his sidewalk.

Well, at least he, Margie, and the girls had gotten to thaw out for ten months in Alabama while he attended Air Command and Staff College at Maxwell Air Force Base.

With Montgomery's stultifying heat and humidity, it had been an "ice-to-fire" climate change that had taken a good deal of getting used to, but on balance ACSC had been a good year.

It had, he knew, come very close to being a truly disastrous year.

He thought back to that painful December day when he intended to use some unexpected time off to surprise his wife and take her to lunch, only to discover his best friend's car in front of his house. The cacophony of conflicting thoughts he had experienced at the sight of Larry's 280Z were still fresh in his mind, despite the full year that had now passed since that particular sensory shock.

His first impulse at the time had been to immediately rush into his house to confront Larry and his wife and find out what the hell was going on. Fortunately, he'd been able to resist that instinct, based in no small part on his vivid recollections of an especially gruesome double homicide case he'd prosecuted when he was in Alaska. That case had involved a young buck sergeant whose enraged reaction to discovering his wife in bed with another G.I. had been to use his shotgun to resolve the problem. That particular aggrieved husband now resided in Fort Leavenworth, where he'd have the next thirty years to assess the wisdom of his spontaneous response to the most primal of marital affronts.

Intuitively, Jack had instantly realized that the next few minutes could radically alter the direction of the rest of his life, and thus decided to drive past his house to the park three blocks further at the end of the street in order to collect himself before doing anything. He had to think things through at least a little bit before he acted, he knew.

He had parked facing westward so that he could still see Larry's sports car in the distance while he frantically tried to figure out what to do. *Margie is consummating an affair right now with that son of a bitch who pretends my best friend,* he thought with equal parts fear and rage. *There might just be innocent explanation,* his more cautious inner self immediately countered, though what that might be eluded him at the moment. *Aren't you just afraid of what you'll find out when you go through that door, you gutless wuss,* a third strident inner voice interjected.

The thought that his wife was having an affair and the certainty of the divorce that would follow had knotted his stomach to an extent he'd never before experienced. He panicked at the obvious implications of a divorce at this point in his life. *I can live without Margie,* he had thought angrily, but then immediately felt instant terror when he considered the likelihood of being stationed somewhere halfway around the world from St. Louis. That's where Margie would almost certainly relocate with the kids if they were to split, making any kind of regular visitation worse than impossible. Then his stomach really turned at the thought of some asshole becoming a new father to his girls. And the financial toll would be extreme, necessitating a downward lifestyle drop for both him and his girls – it might even make college impossible for Heather and Cindy. Jack's desperation at the insoluble scenario he had just crafted quickly morphed back into rage as he pictured a sweaty Wilkins on top of his naked wife in his bed in his house.

Why would Margie cheat on me, he lamented to himself – he'd never once cheated on her in all the years they'd been married. *Why would Larry want to screw my wife*? Sure, Larry had always struck him as a bit of a Pepé Le Pew, sniffing around women in general and trying overly hard to be charming, but Jack had always dismissed his flirtatious behavior as nothing more than a harmless personality quirk. After all, Larry's wife Patty was attractive, smart and vivacious, and they seemed happy enough. *I hope the hell she's screwing around herself*, he thought with petty bitterness.

After just a couple minutes of almost uncontrollably frenetic angst-filled mental gymnastics, Jack had actually cooled off enough so that he believed he could handle whatever he discovered behind his front door. Not knowing would be the worst option of all. He'd just restarted his engine when he saw the sports car drive away in the distance.

Jack drove the three blocks back to his house in a little over a minute, using the remote to open the garage door as he pulled in the driveway – it suddenly occurred to him that Margie would now have at least a few seconds advance notice that he was unexpectedly home.

She was in the laundry room starting the washer when he walked in, and expressed surprise at his unexpected arrival. She immediately told him that he had just missed Larry, whom she said had stopped by to drop off a memorandum he was working on and wanted Jack to look at. She'd offered him a cup of coffee, she said – there were in fact two empty coffee cups in the kitchen sink, Jack had noticed. She related that while chatting with her over the joe, the silly guy had realized he was late for a meeting back at Gunter and had to leave in a hurry, forgetting in his haste to take the memorandum out of his briefcase to leave for Jack. She was sure he'd give it to Jack next time they saw each other.

The scenario seemed plausible enough, Jack remembered thinking, since Larry had more than once asked for his help when it came to legal writing – Jack had, after all, been editor of the law review at Northwestern, and although Larry was an exceptionally glib and persuasive orator, he was far less gifted when it came to the written word.

Jack had seen no obvious hint in Margie's matter-of-fact demeanor that she wasn't being straight with him. *Thank God that's all it was,* he had thought.

Given the draining emotional trauma he had manufactured for himself over the preceding few minutes, Jack had not been disappointed when Margie politely declined his impromptu lunch invitation – she said she wasn't feeling all that well. He remembered feeling both immensely relieved and embarrassed . . . relieved that his worst fears were almost certainly baseless and embarrassed for assuming infidelity on her part based on a single piece of highly circumstantial evidence.

The rest of their time in Montgomery had been personally uneventful, and he'd seen nothing else to raise any concerns about the fidelity of their relationship. He wondered why he still continued to think about that December day so often.

He'd completed ACSC last May as a Distinguished Graduate, an honor received by less than 10% of his classmates, and grabbed the proverbial brass ring when he was reassigned as a staff judge advocate – chief attorney – of a Strategic Air Command wing. Being offered such a prestigious leadership gig as a major, earlier than almost all of his contemporaries, was a very big deal professionally. The legal office he now ran was not a big one – his staff consisted of three other young judge advocates, four non-commissioned paralegals, and two civilians (a secretary and a court reporter.) He was nevertheless a SAC SJA, a job he truly loved.

Oscoda, Michigan, two thirds of the way up the eastern side of the state on the shores of Lake Huron, wouldn't have been his first choice (as if he really *had* a choice!) from a purely geographic point of view, but the B-52 wing he served – the 379th Bomb Wing with its nuclear deterrence mission – was an exciting and important place to work. Wurtsmith, he knew, wasn't the only SAC base that was cold and isolated. Most SAC wings, in fact, were scattered throughout the northern tier of the United States in order to be a few minutes closer to the Soviet Union using the most direct flight route, pretty much due north over Canada and the pole, in case they were ever called upon to unleash their fury on behalf of the nation.

To call Oscoda small and remote was to badly understate the matter. The town had one stoplight, two gas stations, a couple Mom & Pop restaurants, a new McDonalds that had just opened last fall with a lot of fanfare, and one theater.

The movie theater was a real hoot – the first arriving patrons were normally first ushered into the lobby until at least 20 were present, at which time the owners would then allow them to take seats and whatever movie was playing would be shown. If less than 20 moviegoers showed up, their money was refunded and they'd be left to find other entertainment for the evening, no small accomplishment in Oscoda. That happened about half the time.

The closest airport was two hours south in Saginaw (a real pain in the rear when he had to go TDY), and the closest K-Mart was an hour north in Alpena, a snowy drive he and Margie had made more than once when they needed something they couldn't find in the Wurtsmith Base Exchange. With gas prices now hovering about $1.40 a gallon, neither trip was made casually. No, this place was not exactly Metropolis. In fact, he thought, it's *probably not even Smallville.*

Well, maybe the Career Management Office would give him that European posting he and Margie coveted so much after they'd paid some "remote assignment" dues here.

Back inside his kitchen, he poured a cup of coffee, threw in a packet *of Sweet and Low*™, and sat down to read the morning newspaper.

The front page was pretty standard for the *Free Press*. A couple of overnight street murders in Motown (*what else was new?*), a feature about some of the auto workers being laid off by Ford (*what else was new?*), and a piece he read that said the Fed was likely to lower the prime interest rate to 12.5% in an attempt to help spur the still sluggish economy.

As he scanned the economic article, which was mostly bad news, he thought to himself that at least things weren't as bad as they were right after Carter left office, when the inflation rate had spiked at over 13% and the prime rate got to over 20%. Thankfully, inflation was now down to a somewhat more manageable annual rate of around 8%, though still far in excess of the 4% pay raise military members had received each of the last two years. He, and almost everyone else in the country he presumed, was still losing ground.

At least he was still working. The article pointed out that while inflation had been reduced significantly, the American unemployment rate had gone the other direction, having been stuck right at 10% for the past couple of years. No wonder that the Republicans had had their butts so thoroughly kicked last November and a Democrat was now sitting in the Oval Office, thought Kuhn.

Just as he was about to pour another cup of coffee – *better make another pot before Margie gets up* – the phone rang. One of the downsides of his current job was being subject to phone calls at any hour of the day, weekdays and weekends alike, whenever anything seriously untoward happened on base. When his home phone rang between 2300 in the evening and 0700 in the morning or during the weekend, the odds were high that it wasn't a social call.

As he suspected, the voice on the other end of the phone belonged to Lieutenant Colonel John Pulaski, Wurtsmith's chief of security police. The nature of their respective jobs meant that Pulaski and Kuhn got the chance to work together a lot – Kuhn liked Pulaski, particularly his straight-shooting, albeit frequently crude, way of looking at things. What you saw with him was what you got, with no frills or pretensions. As Wurtsmith's top cop, Pulaski had two missions in life – protection of the wing's nukes and law enforcement within the base's fence line – and he took those two missions *very* seriously. He and his people were very good at both of them.

"They're baaaack," were Pulaski's first words after identifying himself, his rough voice doing a poor but passable imitation of the famous line from the movie *Poltergeist*.

"You're kidding," replied Kuhn, pretty sure that the cop was referring to the small group of Catholic anti-nuclear activists from Saginaw, some of them nuns, who made occasional weekend sojourns north to Wurtsmith to vent their collective spleens. The anti-nuke movement seemed to be ramping up nationwide, Jack knew, but those targeting his base had been especially persistent.

"No, I'm not," said Pulaski, who then told him that about a dozen protestors, including that "lard-ass nun" had just attempted to cut through a section of fence about a hundred yards north of the main gate. Pulaski, who was Catholic himself, had virtually boundless disdain for those who misused their positions in *his* church to engage in radical – and stupid – political stunts, particularly when those stunts gave aid and comfort to America's enemies.

"Pretty ballsy," answered Kuhn, "since we now have a restraining order." Major Kuhn had personally worked that one, appearing in Federal Court in Saginaw to convince a judge to issue an injunction against any further trespasses by Sister Beatrice Dalton and her merry band of protestors.

What had persuaded the judge was the group's last foray up north to Oscoda, during which they had thrown a balloon filled with red paint (representing blood, of course) at the main gate shack, splattering, though not injuring, two SP guards then on duty. Though the judge had not given members of the group any jail time, he had fined them each $500, and suspended a three-day jail sentence. More importantly from the SJA's view, he had issued an order directing them to henceforth stay at least a thousand feet away from the perimeter of Wurtsmith.

"No kidding," replied Pulaski, "I think it's a good day to throw some nuns in the can."

"You know, by the way," he continued, "that the SAC regulation says we have to strip-search any potential terrorist that we catch trying to forcibly enter the base."

"Oh really? I doubt very much that it's referring to wacko nuns," said Kuhn, really hoping that the head cop was just pulling his chain – Jack couldn't always tell with Pulaski.

"The reg doesn't differentiate on the basis of their day jobs," Pulaski replied a little too curtly to suit Kuhn. The SJA didn't like the direction this conversation seemed to be heading.

"Are you telling me that your folks have already conducted full body cavity inspections?" asked Jack, fearing the answer he shortly received.

"That's what I'm telling you," the head cop replied. "The night shift flight chief knows what the SAC regulation says, and he followed it."

"Please tell me at least that they were conducted by same gender cops," Jack groaned.

"Of course, Jack," answered Pulaski, "we're not complete idiots."

"O.K., I'll be right over," said Kuhn, immediately starting to mentally catalogue the myriad possible repercussions . . . awful public relations, lots of holier than thou higher headquarters second-guessing, and, very likely, highly political lawsuits from the "violated" protestors.

With that, Jack hung up the phone, emptied his coffee cup in the sink, and made a beeline for the bedroom to throw his uniform on. *Just another day in the defense of America,* he thought sarcastically to himself.

CHAPTER 8

The White House, Washington, D.C.
7:15 a.m., March 29, 1985

The red and white cover of the thick file Walter Mondale picked up off his Oval Office desk read *"TOP SECRET: POTUS EYES ONLY."* Though he had loathed wading through the innumerable government files that crossed his desk when he was a Senator and later Vice President, this one was different – it had been built at his very specific order. He resolved to at least get through the executive summary before beginning another unspeakably hectic day, one he knew would once again be chock full of too many people and too many things to do.

He skimmed the terse introduction:

From: National Security Advisor
Re: Foreign Policy and Defense

Introduction: This memorandum responds to your direction that we provide you recommendations fully vetted and coordinated with the National Security Council (NSC) and the White House (WH) senior staff concerning those areas of foreign policy and defense policy most in need of change from the previous administration.

It was a big job he'd asked his NSA to undertake, specifically to prepare a comprehensive foreign policy vision for the new Administration. Because his foreign policy options were, he knew, inexorably intertwined with the current economic challenges facing this country, he had unambiguously instructed his NSA to take domestic matters into consideration in building that vision.

As a veteran Washington insider and consummate political survivor - he had, after all, continued to prosper politically in spite of his four years of VP duties with the unpopular Jimmy Carter - Mondale knew the critical importance of setting priorities that resonated with the electorate. His 1984 campaign had focused almost exclusively on economic issues, and specifically his promise to at long last overcome the long-term economic doldrums that had now persisted through the administrations of three straight presidents, two now discredited and one dead.

Consistent with his campaign pledge, he had made the profoundly expensive but eminently necessary American Economic Recovery Act, containing a robust menu of new job-creation, vocational training, and unemployment benefit initiatives, the first and top priority of his administration. AERA had been enacted at breathtaking speed by an unusually friendly and compliant Congress only five weeks after his inauguration. The downside, of course, was the resultant significant deepening of the overall federal budget deficit, a matter that he knew would impact his options when it came to foreign and defense policy decisions. The good news, he thought, was that his counterpart in Moscow was undoubtedly having to juggle guns and butter in exactly the same way.

Mondale began to read the first paragraph, titled "Strategic Considerations":

Nuclear Strategy: Though the term is clearly politically unacceptable and should not be used by the Administration in any public pronouncements, the fact of the matter is that the concept of Mutual Assured Destruction (MAD) has kept the peace between the Soviet Union and the United States for nearly forty years, and promises to continue to do so for the foreseeable future. Given that both nations currently possess nuclear arsenals capable of annihilating every person on earth several times over, and recognizing that Premier Gorbachev is also struggling to deal with troublesome budgetary shortfalls, we believe there now exists a unique window of opportunity to seriously pursue truly meaningful mutual reductions. Such reductions would clearly be "win-win" for America and the Soviet Union, who both currently have a strong incentive to reduce military expenditures where possible. There is, we are convinced, a good deal of wiggle room – it is the sense of the NSC that America could unilaterally reduce its nuclear inventory by 75% without any risk whatsoever. While it would not be prudent to pre-announce unilateral reductions in the American nuclear arsenal, we believe that the time is right to publicly challenge the Soviets to convert the upcoming Strategic Arms LIMITATION Talks into REDUCTION negotiations, the vehicle to make massive cuts to both nations' inventories. Further, given the imminent need to begin to slow the increase in the federal deficit, we also believe the cost savings from those likely reductions should be immediately factored in the Five-Year Defense Plan budget process.

Mondale smiled approvingly. His team had gotten this issue right as rain – there was a unique window of opportunity here, and he was sure as hell going to take it. He thought it likely that Gorbachev would too. More to come, he thought, and turned back to the executive summary.

Missile Defense: Your opponent in the last election made much of his proposal to develop and rapidly deploy a space-based anti-ballistic missile defense program. During your second debate with Senator Dole, of course, you decisively (according to our issue-specific polling) pointed out the folly of his proposal – its reliance on wholly unproven technology, the impossibility of ever assuring 100% protection, the fact that such a program would be viewed as a dangerous provocation by both the Soviets and the Chinese, and the irresponsible diversion of huge amounts of dollars badly needed for social programs and other higher priority defense needs. Nevertheless, since Senator Nunn has supported some level of research and development in this area, and since his support as Chairman of the Senate Armed Services Committee will be critical to the Administration's various other defense initiatives, it may now be prudent to stake out more of a middle ground position on this issue and propose minimal research and development funding (in the neighborhood of $50 million per year) as a hedge against future potential threat scenarios. The

NSC also recommends, however, that quiet back-channel assurances be given to the Soviets and the Chinese that America has no present plans to actually build or deploy such a system.

Mondale grimaced, chafing at the prospect of throwing any money at all at what he knew was ludicrous pie-in-the-sky science fiction of the worst kind – a space-based Maginot line that promised to be every bit as porous and ineffective as the original French version. Nevertheless, his NSA knew Nunn well, and was probably right in recommending that the senior Senator from Georgia not be overtly disrespected on this issue by the new Administration. *Well, maybe we could earmark a little seed money for R&D*, he thought, though he was pretty sure he'd be able to convince Nunn to be satisfied with something less than the report recommended, maybe in the neighborhood of $25-30M. At any rate, so long as the Soviets understood that America wasn't really serious about building a missile defense system, there'd probably be little harm. And in the scheme of things, thirty million dollars was not really very much political pork, particularly if it bought the goodwill of a heavyweight like Nunn.

Mondale turned to the next page, captioned "Specific Geographic Area Concerns."

Europe: There are considerable dollar savings to be harvested by significantly drawing down U.S. military presence in Western Europe, thereby forcing the relatively prosperous nations of that continent to finally shoulder a proportionate share of the burden of their defense. Although European troop reductions have been continuously debated for well over a decade, it is the NSC's considered opinion that American troop strength in the European theater can now be reduced by two-thirds (approximately 200,000 personnel) over the next five years without any significant risk to vital American interests. That assessment is based upon the fact that the Soviet military will continue to be stretched very thin by the requirement to support both long-term Afghanistan operations and robust operational demands in the area of internal security, particularly regarding the Soviet

Union's southern republics. It should also be apparent that the Soviets have no interest in occupying and/or ravaging the nations of Western Europe at a time when those nations are becoming increasingly important as trading partners. Additionally, the Helsinki Accords, which among other things legally ratified the post-WWII boundaries of the Warsaw Pact nations, removed a major irritant to the Soviet Union, thus further militating against the premise that the Soviets have any military designs upon or ambitions toward Western Europe.

Pulling back from Europe was going to be dicey and controversial, Mondale intuitively knew, but the report's recommendation to sharply reduce American troop presence in the European theater was something he long ago became convinced needed doing. There was simply too much money involved in continuing to provide the bulk of defense needs for a continent full of countries who were now, in many cases, more economically well off than America. He knew that assumptions regarding an adversary's true intentions were always fraught with uncertainty, and hoped like the dickens that history would confirm his underlying premise of Soviet disinterest in direct European conquest. It made sense to him, and did to his NSA and NSC as well. He returned to reading.

<u>Middle East:</u> *As the bombing of the Marine barracks in Beirut a year and a half ago and the failure of the Desert One hostage rescue attempt in Iran in 1980 so convincingly demonstrated, any use of American military in the volatile Middle East is unlikely to end in success and thus should be assiduously avoided if at all possible. Indeed, it is frankly difficult to conceive any scenario in that troubled region where the deployment of U.S. combat forces would make sense. Rather, we believe that the far better course of action is to continue to count on Israel to "police" this region and protect American interests – the United States should continue its robust support, both publicly and privately, of the state of Israel and its military forces. With regard to hostile nations in the Middle East outside Israel's effective sphere of direct military influence, specifically Iran, we believe*

that quiet but substantial support of Iraq's continuing combat operations against Iran may be the best method of pursuing America's need to contain Tehran and the brand of aggressive religious-political fundamentalism it fosters. While Iraqi president Saddam Hussein is no great respecter of human rights and can be relatively ruthless when he views it necessary, the same could be said of many other Middle Eastern heads of state (e.g., Nasser and Sadat of Egypt, King Hussein of Jordan, and the former Shah of Iran) with whom we have historically cooperated when it served American interests. Having said that, it is obviously important that American support of Iraq remain covert.

Saddam Hussein, Mondale thought sarcastically, now there's a wonderful ally. Such was life, however, when it came to dealing with the Arab world, a region where democracy had never been able to take root and iron-fisted despots were the rule rather than the exception. Again, he silently agreed with the analysis of his NSA – the only viable foreign policy approach was continued public support of Israel and ultra-private support of whatever Arab government could, at any given time, serve American interests. Fortunately, Mondale knew that this principle of expedient "transitory coalitions" – no doubt a legacy of the Arabs' wandering Bedouin roots – was the basis for foreign policy decisions for almost all Middle East governments as well. Mondale also knew that the Arab world needed a viable America as a customer as badly as the U.S. needed the Arabs' oil.

Mondale continued to scan the rest of the report's region-by-region tour of the globe, mentally paraphrasing and silently endorsing its recommendations. He quickly passed through Korea (*don't repeat President Carter's mistake by precipitously announcing U.S. troop reductions in South Korea. . . North Korean dictator-for-life Kim Il Sung's ambitions and intentions remain uncertain*); Japan (*explore reducing the American military footprint, particularly in Okinawa*); China (*continue to expand economic ties and adhere to a "one-China" diplomatic policy*); and sub-Saharan Africa (*no change in the current largely hands-off approach*) until he reached the region he was particularly interested in at the very end of the executive summary. He read this section more carefully.

Caribbean Basin: This critical area of the world has, in our view, been badly neglected for many years. Specifically, as you propounded so effectively during the 1984 campaign, U.S. negligence and focus on other areas of the world over the last several years has directly contributed to the emergence of an overtly anti-American "Axis" (currently consisting of Cuba, Nicaragua, El Salvador, Grenada, and arguably Panama) that now exists to our immediate south. While we do not propose you yet publicly endorse regime-change in these countries, we do believe it is essential to focus much more U.S. attention and resources on those other countries in the Caribbean basin, Central America, and South America which appear to be most vulnerable to the growing influence of Cuba and its new allies in this hemisphere. Of immediate concern are the currently friendly governments of Jamaica, Honduras, Costa Rica, Venezuela, Columbia, Peru, and most importantly Mexico. The United States must do whatever is necessary – economically, politically, and militarily – to support and where necessary shore up the pro-American governments in those Western Hemisphere nations struggling with rebel movements associated with the Cuban-led axis. In that regard, we believe that some of the savings realized from the expected drawdown of our nuclear arsenal and significant reduction of our troop strength in Europe should be re-channeled to dramatically increase American military "special operations" capabilities. Such capability will be absolutely critical not only to the success of America's efforts to curb further growth in the number of hostile regimes in the Western Hemisphere, but also to prevent another military disaster like that which occurred at "Desert One" during the abortive 1980 rescue attempt of the American hostages in Iran.

Yes, yes, yes, Mondale thought, the Caribbean basin is the key. The volatile region directly to America's south was, Mondale knew, was both the primary product source and principal smuggling route for the exponentially exploding cocaine scourge that now posed such a serious threat to America's well-being. Further, Castro's abrasive brand of anti-American communism had been allowed to migrate off his island nation to infect other nations in the region while the United States' gaze and attention had been elsewhere. Just as importantly, unlike a lot of other areas in the world thought Mondale, making a difference in America's backyard was potentially "do-able."

Mondale knew, of course, that making progress in the Caribbean would require both sticks and carrots. The question of which tool to use with regard to Nicaragua was particularly vexing, particularly since the leftist Sandinistas currently in power were almost certainly no worse than the corrupt pro-American Somoza government they'd overthrown a few years back. Some of the President's advisors, and some serious players on the Hill, thought there was still opportunity to proactively turn the Sandinistas away from Fidel, principally through the application of considerable American aid dollars. Mondale would have to think more about that one.

At the bottom line, however, the new President was content with his now crystallized foreign policy vision. If he could win some battles in the War on Drugs, contain Cuba's influence in the Western Hemisphere, ratchet down a Cold War that every rational thinker on both sides knew was "unwinnable," and substantially reduce America's massive military budget in the process, he'd be remembered as one of the greatest chief executives who ever served his country. And, he knew in his heart, America and the world would be a better and a safer place.

CHAPTER 9

Southern Oklahoma

2130 hours, 30 June 1987

As he barreled southward down Interstate 35, a good deal in excess of the 55 mph speed limit, Jack Kuhn mused to himself that he must have been a truck driver in a previous life. He really did enjoy an occasional solitary long-distance drive – "Teamster therapy" he had once described it to Margie – particularly when traffic was as light as it was this evening. At this speed, he'd make it to Carswell Air Force Base in Fort Worth, and the fourteen-dollar-a-night visiting officers room (VOQ) he'd reserved there, by midnight.

He bought this car, a used maroon 1979 Oldsmobile Cutlass Supreme, when he'd gotten to Michigan two years ago. It was relatively comfortable, went fast enough to suit him, got OK gas mileage (almost 19 mpg on the open road), and most importantly it was already paid for. He and his wife occasionally talked about maybe getting something newer, but so long as the Olds was running reasonably well, they'd agreed it was best to defer a new vehicle – and the monthly car payments that would go with it – for as long as they could.

He'd said a temporary goodbye to Margie and the girls this morning – they'd be staying with her folks in St. Charles, Missouri just outside St. Louis for the rest of the summer while he got started at his new assignment at Bergstrom Air Force Base in Austin. With a little luck, the base house they'd been promised would be ready by the middle of August, before the school year started in Texas.

Kuhn loved his family, of course, but he also had to admit that he did not relish being cooped up with them in the claustrophobically close quarters of their auto during the marathon cross-country trips that were an occupational hazard of being reassigned every few years. The fact that the girls were a little older – Heather was now 14 and Cindy 12 – made such group journeys indisputably less stressful than the excruciating "trips from Hell" they'd endured earlier in his career when the kids were younger and made the back seat of the car their own private war zone. There were, nevertheless, still three female bladders to contend with when they traveled as a foursome, which translated into annoyingly extended – at least from his point of view – pit stops every hour or two.

As a result, it had taken the family two full days to drive the slightly less than 700 mile distance from Oscoda to his in-laws' house. This day, on the other hand, he'd already driven 600 miles, and was now less than two hours away from his planned destination for the evening.

Realizing that he was sufficiently desensitized to the "John Denver's Greatest Hits" eight-track he'd now listened to several times through, he pulled out the bulky black cassette, threw it on the empty seat beside him, and began fiddling with the radio dial to find something else to listen to. Finding little but the tell-tale twangy lyrics of one country music station after another, interspersed with the instantly recognizable moralizing of the ubiquitous Christian stations in this area of the country, he quickly decided that some silence might not be a bad thing. He turned the radio off.

That's better, he concluded. His mind, now freed from auditory distractions, wandered back to the tour of duty he'd just completed.

He'd miss Wurtsmith some, he knew, even if he'd hated the cold and never-ending snow-shoveling duties that were integral parts of the long northern Michigan winters. In spite of the wholly inhospitable semi-arctic climate, he thought it was a shame that the base would be closing next year. The Air Force just last month had announced that three of its bomb wings – Wurtsmith and K.I Sawyer Air Force Bases in Michigan and Loring Air Force Base in Maine – would be deactivated by the end of 1988. Some small number of the B-52s stationed at those three bases were to be reassigned to other SAC units, the rest sent off to the boneyard in the desert near Davis-Monthan AFB in Arizona.

It wasn't just bases that were being jettisoned, he knew. People were being aggressively forced out of service as the Air Force's authorized end strength continued to decrease. The reasonably attractive financial incentives that the military had offered folks to leave active duty hadn't been enough, he remembered, requiring the Air Force to conduct a painful "reduction-in-force" board late last year. It had been the first such RIF board since the drawdown right after the Vietnam War. A couple of very good JAGs he knew well had been unfortunate enough to be selected to leave, including a good buddy from law school, Major Paul Hempel, at F.E. Warren AFB in Wyoming. His old friend Larry Wilkins, on the other hand, had not only survived the RIF, but had been selected to participate in the prestigious ASTRA (Air Staff Training Honors Program) program in the Pentagon where he'd be showcased as a serious up-and-comer and work in a variety of JAG Air Staff offices to learn up close and personal how military business is conducted inside the beltway. Jack could only imagine how ecstatically pleased Larry must have been when his selection was publicly announced.

Now that Larry was single again – Patty had suddenly and surprisingly, at least to Jack, left Larry and filed for divorce about a year ago – he was sure the ambitious and personable Major Wilkins would take DC by storm. He involuntarily and physically shuddered as he suddenly remembered that December day in Montgomery when he came so close to irretrievably torpedoing both their lives and careers – that almost certainly would have been the outcome had he chosen to act on what he now knew to have been a baseless assumption about Larry and Margie.

Too depressing and scary a subject, he thought. He decided instead to mentally review the "highlights" of the assignment he'd just completed – God knows he'd been kept almost inhumanly busy at

Wurtsmith. He ticked off in his mind the litany of challenges the legal office there had dealt with under his watch. Several dozen court-martials, including the big drug bust last year. The hundreds of angry claimants his office had to deal with when a contractor (*lowest bidder, of course*!) spray painting the base's water tower failed to take into account that the prevailing north wind would also spray paint a parking lot full of cars, vans, and pick-up trucks. The difficult and politically-charged negotiations with the state and federal environmental zealots regarding cleanup of a trichloroethylene plume which had slowly migrated since being dumped from an aircraft wash rack in the 1950s – it had polluted an underground aquifer that fed into several off-base wells and a recreational lake over a mile from the installation. The more and more frequent anti-nuke protests, mostly outside the main gate, but also one unfortunate case during last year's annual open house, when a half dozen crazies had taken hammers out of their jackets to furiously beat and dent a B-52 on static display on the flight line.

He and his lawyers had worked closely with the U.S. Attorney in Saginaw to get 30-day jail sentences for each of the hammer-wielders, including the omnipresent Sister Beatrice. It was the second time he'd helped put her in the can – she'd been slapped with three days of confinement a couple of months earlier on a trespass and violating a restraining order rap. Jack was still amazed that neither she nor her attorney had raised the issue of the full body cavity search she received courtesy of the Security Police on that earlier occasion. Maybe she viewed the personal intrusion as a badge of honor demonstrating her *bona fides* as a really serious protestor, he thought perversely.

Kuhn's work dealing with the anti-nuke protests had made him the object of some ribbing from his peers. At last year's Strategic Air Command legal conference in Omaha, he'd been referred to by Brigadier General Lacey, SAC's chief lawyer, as the "scourge of nuns everywhere." He had taken the left-handed compliment in the good-natured spirit that Lacey had intended – Kuhn knew that SAC's leadership had been more than satisfied with the way he had handled the protestor problem.

Yep, it had been an action packed two years, highlighted by the grade of "Outstanding" his legal office had been awarded by the usually stingy and always feared SAC inspectors during the last Operational Readiness Inspection – ORI – of the Wurtsmith wing. And though promotions had slowed considerably throughout the Air Force the past couple of years, the promotion gods had recently smiled on Kuhn – he'd been selected for early advancement to lieutenant colonel by last year's board and was now wearing his new silver leaf insignia a full year earlier than he might reasonably have expected.

He and Margie had hoped the impressive inspection grade and below-the-zone promotion would convince the JAG detailers to give him the European assignment they both so badly wanted, but ultimately didn't get. Actually, the JAG assignment folks weren't the problem. The real problem was that the Air Force's bases in Europe were being closed down at the speed of heat, going from over 30 just a few years ago to just under a dozen now, and probably only three or four in another year or two. *Crappy timing on my part*, he lamented to himself, not for the first time.

The assignment to Headquarters Twelfth Air Force to which he was now heading was not a bad consolation prize. He was, for starters, reasonably sure it didn't snow much in Austin. Even more importantly, he was going to a terrific job – Deputy Staff Judge Advocate for a Tactical Air Command Numbered Air Force and its eleven subordinate wings around the country. His new boss would be a JAG full colonel. And as the number two lawyer at the headquarters, he knew he'd be getting to spend a lot of quality time with Lieutenant General Michael "Irish Mickey" Casey, the three-star general who commanded Twelfth Air Force.

Kuhn was really looking forward to working for Casey again. He had first met the F-4 pilot when he was the Wing Commander at Elmendorf. Then *Colonel* Casey was by far the best leader Kuhn had ever seen, a rugged "Steve Canyon" persona brimming with infectious confidence and possessed of great intellect and extraordinary motivational skills. People busted their butts for Casey . . . and liked doing it. Obviously, the Air Force had liked him too, given his rapid accumulation of stars over the past few years.

The Twelfth Air Force mission, Jack knew, included serving as the air component for United States Southern Command, whose area of responsibility included all of Central and South America. Based on Jack's assessment of things, that AOR was quickly becoming "where the action was."

Kuhn glanced at his dashboard display and noticed his gas gauge was now under a quarter of a tank – no great surprise since he hadn't stopped for the last four hours. *Time for a break*, he thought, and began to pay attention to the signs along the side of the interstate to find a place to pit.

He found what he was looking for about ten minutes later, a few miles north of Ardmore. It was a small station – just two pumps – sitting by itself only a few hundred yards west of the interstate. As he pulled next to the first pump, he noticed an old Chevy Impala, which had clearly been around significantly longer than his own aging Cutlass, parked right next to the door of the station. Although the lighting wasn't great, he noticed a woman sitting behind the steering wheel – *probably sent her husband in for a pack of cigarettes*, Kuhn deduced.

Kuhn turned back to his business, wincing at the price of unleaded on the pump. $1.89, as high as up North – Jack had hoped that gas prices might be lower in a place like Oklahoma where they actually pumped the oil out of the ground. *So much for that brilliant economic theory*!

Doing the quick math in his head, he calculated that eight dollars would buy enough petrol to easily get him to Carswell tonight. He'd fill up the tank tomorrow morning at the base gas station there, where the price might be a few cents cheaper a gallon, before heading south on the final leg of his long trip.

He had just inserted the nozzle in the tank when he was startled by a loud *kaboom* that seemed to come from inside the station. Turning his eyes toward the sound, he froze for an instant as he saw a man wearing a ski mask bolt out the front door. Kuhn realized almost at once what was happening, and instinctively dropped to the ground behind his vehicle.

From his only semi-protected position, his military training started to kick in – he quickly began to scan his surroundings to look for some better cover in case he had to make a break. Before he could settle on a potential escape route, however, he heard a car door slam and the sound of wheels spinning on the gravel in front of the station.

Keeping his own car between himself and where its sound told him the getaway car was, he peered over the trunk in time to the see the back end of the car accelerating onto the road and disappearing west into the darkness. The lack of lighting and the dust the car had kicked up made it impossible to read the license plate, or even tell if the car had a license plate for that matter. He wasn't going to be a very useful witness, he realized.

Standing up cautiously, he gathered his composure for a second or two, and then started to walk purposefully toward the front door of the station, dreading what he was afraid he might find inside.

Reaching the glass door in just a few quick steps, he was both surprised and relieved to see a haggard looking old man rise up from behind the counter, a phone receiver in his hand.

"You OK?" Jack blurted as he walked in.

"Yeah," said the man in a shaky voice, "Callin' 911 right now."

Jack then flinched as a chunk of ceiling tile fell just in front of him, splatting as it hit the hard floor. He looked up and saw a large raggedy hole in the ceiling above him, and about the same time felt something loose – like BBs he thought – under his right foot. *Buckshot*, he instantly intuited.

After a relatively short conversation with the police dispatcher, the clerk hung up the phone, and turned back to Jack. "Third time we've been robbed in the last goddamn year. These punks think it's easier to rob someone rather than to get a job. I tell you, I'm too old for this crap."

Jack nodded agreement.

A squad car arrived a few minutes later. It was another hour or so before Jack's statement, first orally to the cop and then a signed handwritten version, was completed. "Not very helpful, I'm afraid," Kuhn apologized to the patrolman.

A few minutes later, the Okie cop told Jack he was free to go. Having finally gotten around to gassing up the car and making a much-needed latrine stop – both to relieve himself and to wash up the scrapes on his forearms from when he'd hit the gravelly deck during all the hubbub – he drove off back toward I-35.

Hell of a pit stop, he thought as he merged back on the southbound interstate, *and a hell of way to start a new assignment.* Although he was a military man, he had never been much of a fan of gunshots in his personal vicinity. He hoped the bizarre events of the last couple hours weren't an omen.

CHAPTER 10

Crystal City, Virginia
0430, 5 December 1987

As he slowly opened his eyes, Major Larry Wilkins groggily struggled to remember where he was. It wasn't until he turned his head to the left and saw the outline of the naked woman still asleep next to him that the fogginess began to clear.

Her name was Noreen he now recalled (or was it Doreen?) and he was in her bed in a small apartment in a Crystal City high-rise. She'd been in a group of Department of Energy civilian secretaries who worked in the Forrestal Building in L'Enfant Plaza who decided to end their workweek yesterday evening enjoying happy hour at the Fort McNair Officers Club. As his consciousness further returned, he remembered how he'd struck up a conversation, then asked her to dance, then bought her a couple of tequila sunrises, and then ultimately "cut her from the herd" by offering her a ride home. She'd invited him in when they arrived at her apartment, and almost immediately began the frenzied foreplay that ended up in her bedroom.

Larry could tell from her alcohol-induced snoring that she was still sound asleep, which greatly facilitated the surreptitious exit he knew from experience was best in these circumstances, since he had absolutely no intent to ever see her again. He stealthily got out of bed, gathered up his uniform and shoes (he'd gotten in the useful habit in these situations of putting all his clothes in a discreet and easily retrievable pile) and quietly got quickly dressed in the still dark living room. In less than three minutes, he was in the elevator heading down to the parking lot next to the apartment building. He was soon driving south on I-395 in his 280Z – at this time of day on a Saturday, it would only take fifteen minutes to cross the Woodrow Wilson Bridge, then head north on I-295 on the other side of the Potomac River to Bolling Air Force Base, where he was staying in Visiting Officers Quarters during the first couple months of his ASTRA assignment. He'd soon have to find more permanent off-base quarters, but after last night he was certain it wouldn't be in the Crystal City high-rise he'd just left.

God, I love DC, Wilkins thought as he crossed the Bridge. Not only did Washington offer the inestimable opportunity of being able to connect up close and personal with the senior officers who were so important to his career master plan, but also allowed him to size up some of his most talented peers and find the weaknesses he might someday need to exploit when it was time in a few years to compete with them for the top position he intended to reach in the Air Force JAG Corps.

Not to mention that getting laid in this town was like shooting fish in the proverbial barrel.

Based on the DoD sticker on Larry's car, the young security policeman on duty at the main gate waved him through without even checking his ID, and within three minutes he was "home" in the small Visiting Officers Quarters (VOQ) room he currently occupied right across the street from the Officers Club. After brewing a cup of Joe in the mini-coffee maker that sat on the mini-refrigerator, he sat down in the room's single easy chair, a threadbare oldie with uncomfortable wooden armrests, situated at the foot of his bed in the 10'x12' room that currently functioned as his living room, dining room and kitchen.

He grabbed the locked burgundy day-planner that sat on the small end-table next to the chair, unlocked it, and opened it to an untitled note page in the back. The page contained a handwritten numbered list of 22 female names. Picking up a pen, he added "23. Doreen ?, DC, Dec 88" to the list. He smiled as he reviewed the first of his previous entries – the name was that of the foxy ice-skater in Colorado Springs to whom he had lost his virginity during a weekend furlough his third year at the Academy. Allowing himself to relive the details of that sexual encounter for a satisfying moment, he was also uber-embarrassed by fact that he hadn't "lost his cherry" until he was 21 years old. He consoled himself in the knowledge that he was doing a pretty good job making up for lost time.

Wilkins had grown up in the small community of Hanover, Indiana, the only child of what he now understood to be a hopelessly low-class and dysfunctional couple. He hated the recurring memory of his frequently unemployed, heavy drinking, and philandering father working intermittent stints for the local garbage disposal company in town, while his mother slaved away as a cook in the high school cafeteria by day and moonlighted as a bartender at the sleezy "Trackside Bar" several nights a week. He'd realized at a very young age that his family occupied the very bottom rung of the economic and prestige ladder of his blue-collar hometown. That fact had been understood by his classmates in school, he remembered, particularly the good-looking and popular high school girls who spurned his every advance when his adolescent hormones began to kick in. He still despised every one of those pompous divas who had refused to have anything to do with him.

Wilkins hated virtually everything about his childhood, but remembered the gradual epiphany he'd begun to experience at 14 reading biographies at the local library. He'd always been a very good student and a voracious reader, for him the only available means of escaping his depressing daily circumstances. He particularly loved stories about historical figures who had risen far above their initially assigned stations in life . . . he was especially fascinated by accounts of the life of Julius Caesar, whose ruthless "do-anything-to-succeed" mentality had resulted in immense power and riches and all the perks that came with them, including the wide array of women who were available to rich and powerful men. The fact that Caesar was a military man also resonated with Wilkins. With the Vietnam War raging on with no end in sight, military service had been almost a certainty for Hanover lads who didn't go to college – several of his drafted classmates only slightly older than him had already returned home from Vietnam in coffins. And since his ne'er-do-well parents would never be able to afford college expenses for their only son, he knew he had to find another way. The Air Force Academy had been the answer, allowing him to avoid dangerous service in Vietnam for at least four years, get a college degree, and earn an officer's commission. And even if he had to eventually go to Vietnam, he reasoned, the Air Force was the military service least likely to expose him to enemy fire, at least as long as he stayed out of a cockpit.

Based on his strong academic record and high standardized test scores, his application had resonated with his local Congressman, himself an Air Force veteran who fortuitously had been born and raised in Hanover – Larry received a much sought after Congressional appointment to the Air Force Academy in Colorado Springs.

His four years at the Academy had truly been life changing. No longer was he an impoverished untouchable from the proverbial "wrong side of the tracks." Instead, he was now one of America's elite, a young lieutenant-to-be upon whom the country would depend in the years and decades to come. He had, of course, significantly altered the embarrassing details of his personal biography for the benefit of his classmates. Whenever pressed to discuss his parents, he described them as successful former restaurant owners who now sadly were both in ill health, which explained their absence at any Academy functions (Parents' Day, football games, graduation, etc.) normally attended by proud dads and moms of USAFA cadets. The only cadet who had ever questioned him and seriously attempted to peel back the onion of his parental narrative was his nosy third-year roommate, Chad Turner. Interestingly, Cadet Turner himself never graduated, having been dismissed at the end of his third year after being unable to completely refute several anonymous but detailed allegations of honor code violations. The extraordinary power of anonymous complaints was a lesson Wilkins would never forget.

Finishing his cup of coffee, Larry quickly perused the rest of his handwritten conquest list. He stopped at number 16, Margie Kuhn. Margie had wanted to get together with him again after their morning tryst in Montgomery. Although the "wife-of-a-friend" aspect had made that particular encounter especially exciting, he knew how dangerous such an extra-marital relationship involving another JAG's spouse could be to his career, so he never went back for seconds. There were, he knew, ample quantities of other available fish in the barrel for him to shoot.

CHAPTER 11

Vienna, Austria

5:00 p.m., November 30, 1988

Walter Mondale still had trouble looking at Mikhail Gorbachev without feeling like he was gaping at the disconcerting purple birthmark that filled a third of the Soviet premier's forehead. As he prepared to walk into the hall, he resolved to himself that he would not stare, particularly since the glaring TV lights would be highlighting his every nuance.

At the signal of the young woman standing at the door, Mondale entered the large room, while at the same time Gorbachev entered from the other side. An audience of around 200 dignitaries (many were from Austria, America, and Russia, of course, but there were also a sizeable number of ambassadors and various other diplomatic officials from literally every corner of the globe) applauded warmly. Both men met in the middle, behind the ornate table at which Edmund Muskie and Eduord Shevardnadze – the "two Eds" thought Mondale – were already standing. The two heads of state smiled broadly at each other, shook hands for several seconds so that the cameras couldn't possibly miss the genuineness of their greeting, and sat down in the two empty chairs between the two-time American Secretary of State and the Soviet Foreign Minister.

Both Gorbachev and Mondale then put headphones on and directed their attention to the speaker at the podium to their left, the Prime Minister of Austria.

Reading his prepared remarks in German, the Prime Minister started by thanking both men for what he termed their "extraordinary goodwill, exceptional vision, and unflagging dedication to peace." After the requisite amount of effusive personal praise for his two guests, the Prime Minister then began to discuss in some detail the treaty they were about to sign.

"This treaty will do what once seemed impossible," said the Austrian PM. He described how the agreement would reduce the nuclear stockpiles of both American and the Soviet Union by almost two thirds, outlaw multiple warhead (MIRV) systems, require the destruction of existing mobile nuclear delivery systems and prohibit the development of any new such system, and mandate an extraordinarily open verification system that demonstrated a level of trust that had never before existed between the world's two greatest superpowers.

After almost five minutes, the Austrian head of state concluded with apparent sincerity. "On behalf of the people of the entire world, I humbly thank President Mondale and Premier Gorbachev for making this planet we all share inestimably safer."

As diplomatic custom dictated, both Gorbachev and Mondale then made similarly effusive and gentile remarks, then got down to the business of ceremonially signing the strategic arms reduction treaty both so badly needed. There'd be time for some real talk later tonight.

7:30 p.m., November 30, 1988

Having concluded their informal (at least by diplomatic standards) dinner along with about a dozen senior officials from each side, Gorbachev and Mondale excused themselves and went into the sitting room that had been reserved for their use. Only their personal translators went with them.

On the coffee table between the two facing overstuffed chairs was a bottle of cognac and two glasses. Gorbachev took the initiative, picking up the bottle and pouring each about two fingers worth.

"It is a good thing we have done, today, Walter," started the Soviet Premier. "I honestly think we are giving our grandchildren a better world."

"I couldn't agree more, Mikhail," earnestly responded the President. "And I'm very glad we could set aside some time to talk here tonight."

"I as well," replied Gorbachev, "there are always important things to discuss."

Mondale nodded.

"First of all, let me congratulate you again, Walter, on a successful election. I for one am very pleased that I will be able to work with you for another four years."

"Thank you. It was a good bit closer than I would have preferred, but I'm obviously happy with the final result," Mondale smiled.

"I never met Mr. Perot. Why do you think the Republican Party selected someone with no political experience to be your opponent?" asked the Soviet premier.

"I think it mostly had to do with our continuing economic problems, Mikhail. Ross is a damn good businessman who knows a lot about making money. I think the Republicans hoped his business experience would convince voters that he could magically cure our economy. What surprised me was how good a politician he turned out to be."

"He wasn't that good a politician, thank goodness," responded Gorbachev. "May I offer a toast to a successful and prosperous second term for you."

"Thank you very much," said Mondale, and both men sipped from their glasses.

"Politics always seems to get back to economics, doesn't it?" observed the Russian.

"Yes, it sure does," the President agreed. "Fortunately, both our economies seem finally to be doing a little better now."

"I think you are correct," Gorbachev responded, "ours has shown some encouraging signs over the past year, and I know yours has too. What we signed today will help some more."

Mondale nodded, then changed the subject. "I should be offering you congratulations as well, Mikhail, on the resolution of your Afghanistan difficulties. I'm not sure I would have wagered that your war there would have ended so well for you. And I know you are happy to be bringing your combat soldiers back home."

"I am indeed," responded the premier. "It has been long and difficult, but I'm confident that the government there is stable and safe. Almost all of the terrorists and bandits have now left the country, one way or the other."

"Those who escaped went to northeastern Pakistan, I assume?" asked the President.

"That's what our intelligence people say, and I believe them," confided Gorbachev. "We don't think there's more than a few hundred left, and they'll be too busy just trying to survive in those mountains and caves to cause us much trouble now."

Mondale nodded again.

"I need to tell you that I am grateful that you and your government privately understood our need to protect our southern flank from the terrorists," added Gorbachev quietly and sincerely. "At least after your peanut farmer was put out of office."

Mondale nodded again. Although Mondale knew that the Afghan government would be anything but independent of their Soviet sponsors, he also understood why the Soviet Union simply couldn't tolerate a haven for Muslim rebels adjacent to their own largely Muslim southern republics. Jimmy Carter, blinded by his fervor for human rights and ingrained sense of pacifism, had never comprehended the Soviet's frankly pragmatic calculus for invading Afghanistan in 1979 – it's always better to stop a burglar while he's at the house next door rather than waiting and having to face him in your own home.

"We *have* understood, Mikhail, even though we couldn't say so publicly. And I trust you understand that my country has similar needs to protect its own southern flank."

"So long as we are not talking about Cuba, Walter, I do understand," said Gorbachev, knowing that the President was referring to that lout Noriega in Panama. "And with regard to Cuba, I promise you that I will do everything I can to make sure our friend Fidel continues to pose no direct threat to America."

"Thank you, Mikhail. I can see we are of one mind when it comes to cleaning up our own backyards."

Both men stopped talking long enough to finish their drinks. This time it was Mondale who picked up the bottle to refill both.

"I will have only one more, my friend," said the premier.

"I didn't know you had become a teetotaler," chided the President good-naturedly.

"No self-respecting Russian can ever be a teetotaler," responded Gorbachev with his famous self-effacing charm. "But I'll relate to you a recent event that has given me pause when it comes to drinking too much."

"Last month I attended a small dinner party hosted by an old-timer named Yeltsin – he is what you would call the mayor of Moscow."

"After dinner, Yeltsin began toasting," related Gorbachev, "and I with the best of intentions honored each one of his toasts. Two hours later Boris was still toasting and drinking. I, on the other hand, was sick as could be. It took me three days to recover!"

"What struck me, however, was not how much liquor Boris could hold. What I really noticed was how bad he looked – he appears much older than he really is. I fear the old drunk has only a fraction of his liver left – he'll be fortunate if he lives long enough to be able to retire. I, on the other hand, would like to enjoy my retirement for many years whenever it comes."

"Do you have any thoughts on when that might be?" Mondale couldn't resist.

"You at least know that you will be freed from your jail cell in four more years," smiled Gorbachev. "I won't be disappointed if I can escape from mine about the same time."

"To long and prosperous retirements," offered Mondale raising his glass.

And Gorbachev decided that one more drink in the name of diplomatic courtesy probably wouldn't cut too many years off his life.

CHAPTER 12

Bergstrom Air Force Base
Austin, Texas
0620 hours, 16 August 1989

Lieutenant Colonel Jack Kuhn didn't often regard the Austin *American-Statesman* as a legal reference source, but this day it was the best available option – the office wouldn't receive the Supreme Court's full slip opinion from West Publishing Company for several more days.

The headline at the top of the front page of today's edition succinctly summed up yesterday's surprising decision – *Supreme Court Rules Gay Gis Can Serve.* The story below that headline described how the nation's highest court had issued its unexpected opinion in a case involving an Air Force airman basic who had been discharged from the military after revealing to his basic training instructor at Lackland AFB that he was homosexual.

By a 7-2 majority, according to the article, the *Supremes* had ruled that the Department of Defense regulation prohibiting homosexuals from serving in the military was unconstitutional. In a scathing opinion authored by Justice Thurgood Marshall, the story went on, the Court found that the long-standing military policy violated both the Equal Protection Clause and inherent rights of privacy guaranteed by the Constitution. Only associate justices Rehnquist and O'Connor dissented, the article said, further noting that all four of President Mondale's appointees (including Chief Justice John Paul Stevens) joined in the majority opinion concluding that the military policy unlawfully discriminated against gays.

Wow, thought Jack, *that's going to change some things in a hurry.* The place of gays in the military had been debated acrimoniously by polar opposite camps for years now. Those in favor of open service had stridently argued that it was fundamentally a civil rights issue, and that since gays were already serving in the military, albeit in the closet, there would be absolutely no impact on the effectiveness of the armed forces by allowing them to serve openly. Those opposing the change argued that since homosexuality was more about conduct than status, adding openly gay soldiers into the mix of the close quarters living conditions frequently imposed upon military members would irreparably undermine unit discipline and inevitably erode combat readiness.

Jack suspected that, as with many things, the real truth lay somewhere in between those two extremes. Regardless, the Supreme Court's landmark decision had, for all intents and purposes, suddenly ended this particular debate. If Kuhn correctly read between the lines of the newspaper story, by deciding the case on Constitutional grounds the Court had pre-empted (presumably intentionally) any possibility of Congressional action to reverse the decision by new legislation.

There'll be, Jack thought certain, a good deal of initial gnashing of teeth on the part of many in uniform. The JAG was just as certain, however, that the predictable vitriolic backlash would be short-lived. Ultimately, he knew, just about everyone in service understood the need to salute smartly and move on once a decision had been made by the military's civilian masters. And this decision had now been made.

That the Supreme Court decided the issue the way they did wasn't really much of a shock, he reflected. It was, after all, a relatively short leap from their decision announced last year striking down the Georgia statute (and by extrapolation every other such statute throughout the United States) which had criminalized sodomy among consenting adults.

This Court was not at all shy about tackling tough social questions, knew Jack, mentally checking off the subject areas of its major decisions over the past couple of years – abortion rights, lots of search and seizure cases, free speech (particularly in schools), environmental issues, affirmative action, etc., etc., etc. And given the Court's current composition, it was not surprising that its decisions in those contentious areas frequently enraged conservatives and sometimes made proponents of traditional judicial restraint shake their heads in disbelief. Measured against the extraordinary activism of this Court, Kuhn mused thinking back to the cases he'd studied in Constitutional Law back at Northwestern, the Warren Court of the 1950s and 60s was almost comatose by comparison.

And that wasn't likely to change any time soon, Jack knew. With old-timers Burger, Powell, Brennan, and White all having departed over the past four years, Marshall and Blackmun were the only current justices who were really long in the tooth. The other justices were likely to be around to flex their active judicial muscles for a long time to come.

Tossing the *American-Statesman* back into his open briefcase on the side credenza, Lt Col Kuhn reached for this week's edition of the *Air Force Times* at the top of the stack in his in-basket. Scanning the front page, his eye was drawn to a sidebar headline that read *USAF End Strength to Drop Again.* He turned to page 8 to scan the full story.

Congressionally authorized active-duty end strength for the Air Force, the story said, would drop to 385,000 for fiscal year 1990, the story said, a decrease of 30,000 from the previous year. The article also pointed out that total active-duty strength for all the services would drop to roughly 1.2 million by the end of FY90, and noted that the figure represented a drop of about 900,000 – more than 40 percent – over the past decade.

So, what else is new? Jack thought with just a trace of bitterness. He wondered more and more often these days whether the Air Force had been a good career choice, and even if it had been originally, how much longer he ought to hang around given the military's current state of free-fall drawdown. As but one example, it was announced last week that the JAG Corps would be losing two of the its four general officer billets, part of a sweeping Congressionally mandated flag officer reduction throughout all the armed forces.

He knew exactly where Margie stood on the issue – her words and body language were unmistakably clear during a recent semi-civil discussion concerning whether he should opt for the 15-year retirement (with a reduced pension) now being offered by the Air Force to induce sufficient numbers of career officers to voluntarily depart. She adamantly thought it was time . . . indeed past time . . . for him to hang up the blue suit and start earning the kind of money many of his law school classmates practicing in the civilian world were now making.

It was hard to blame her for that point of view, Jack empathized.

Military members had continued to lose ground in their paychecks over the past several years, as their annual raises always seemed to be at least a percentage point or two below inflation, which at least, he thought thankfully, had only been at 6 or 7 percent each of the past four years. There was constant scuttlebutt about an impending "catch-up" raise of between 10 and 30 percent (it depended on who was conveying the scuttlebutt) being right around the corner, but it never seemed to materialize.

Supply and demand being what it was, he suspected, there's little likelihood that anybody would see that kind of pay raise so long as the military services were still trying to get rid of, rather than retain, lots of folks in uniform.

Margie was also tired of being stuck on the bottom teaching rung of the succession of high schools where she taught, she had pointedly told him. He hadn't had a very good answer to that one other than to point out that the gypsy lifestyle – moving to a new place every two or three years – was simply an inescapable fact of life for a military family.

That response had not been smart on his part, Kuhn instantly realized, as he then got an earful from Margie about how much the girls also hated the constant moving, changing schools, and leaving old friends behind. When she added the dreaded "you'd know that if you were home more" line, he knew the conversation was going downhill fast.

In a way, she was right about that too. Another major irritant of the drawdown, Jack and Margie knew from very personal experience, was the increasingly strenuous workload imposed upon those remaining on active duty. He was having to spend more and more time at the office to keep up with his portfolio of responsibilities.

Particularly in the legal business, Jack understood from personal experience that a smaller military did not translate into a smaller workload. In fact, in many areas of legal work, the drawdown generated significant additional work. There were labor cases by civilian DoD employees challenging loss of their federal jobs, continuing litigation challenges to the way the reduction in force and mandatory early retirement boards were being conducted, a spate of complaints (mostly spurious, Jack knew) to the Inspector General from folks hoping to use its "whistleblower" protections as a shield against being separated, lots of procurement protests by civilian contractors fighting hard to get their piece of a smaller defense pie, and huge environmental challenges meeting accelerated clean-up schedules at bases that had been closed or were scheduled to close, to name but a few.

All that notwithstanding, Jack still really enjoyed being a JAG. He loved the diversity of legal challenges he got to face every day, he loved the great people he got to work with, he loved the high level of responsibility he shouldered, and he loved the purity of a law practice unencumbered by the economics of a client's ability to pay and the tyranny of having to generate obscenely huge numbers of "billable hours" for the firm. God knows he worked a lot of hours himself – probably at least 70 a week between the office and the briefcase he took home every night – but the work he was doing was important to the Air Force and the country. And he knew he was doing it very well.

He was relieved when their collective cooler heads had prevailed. Margie hadn't made his getting out a "fall-on-the-sword" issue, though she was visibly disappointed he hadn't taken her counsel. They'd "agreed" that Jack would stay until he had twenty years service and competed for promotion to colonel. *Margie and the girls are real troopers*, Jack thanked his lucky stars.

Kuhn heard footsteps walking down the hallway, and recognized them as belonging to his boss, Colonel Fillman. Jack looked up at the clock – *six thirty, right on time as usual.* Tossing the *Air Force Times* into his out-box, Kuhn decided it was time to get started on today's stack in his in-basket.

CHAPTER 13

The White House, Washington, D.C.
11:45 a.m., December 19, 1989

Having just ushered out his last visitor before lunch, President Mondale turned on the television in the Oval Office to CNN, then hit the mute button to wait for the press conference he knew would be starting shortly in the Quarry Heights compound located in now liberated Panama.

The decision to go to war, he thought, hadn't been as difficult as he thought it would be. Noriega had made it a good deal easier, of course, when his puppet National Assembly displayed the incredibly brazen chutzpah of themselves declaring war on America. The killing of the unlucky American major by Noriega's goons was the final straw, and had convinced Mondale that Christmas season or not, military action against Panama could be delayed no longer.

The corollary decision to take down the Sandinistas in Nicaragua at the same time had required a little more thought, he remembered. Indisputably communist in their outlook and sympathies, Daniel Ortega and his Sandinista government had been a thorn in the American side ever since they deposed Somoza and took power in 1979.

They had, of course, lied to their own people when they promised free elections – ten years had passed and Nicaraguans were still waiting. Of more concern to America, however, was their continued complicity (by serving as a conduit to funnel Cuban-supplied weapons to various rebel groups in the region) in several left-wing insurgencies throughout Central and South America.

The Sandinistas, however, also had their own insurgency at home to worry about. The "Contras" had been pressing the Nicaraguan government hard for several years now, even before Mondale had reinstated significant covert American assistance to the rebels. He'd quietly turned the spigot back on after the CIA had brought him convincing evidence that the Ortega government had blatantly diverted American humanitarian aid dollars to support Cuban-sponsored military mischief throughout the region. The Contras' on-going struggle with the Sandinistas for control of the country was now, for all intents and purposes, a stalemate.

Until the execution-style slaughter in late November of over a hundred men, women, and children – including two American missionaries from Utah – in a small village correctly considered by government forces to be a Contra stronghold, the United States had had no really legitimate basis to intervene directly. That atrocity had been committed by a small squad of Nicaraguan government troops, who were unaware that they were emptying their AK-47 magazines in view of a concealed American photographer with a telephoto lens.

The photographer, Mondale remembered angrily, had been detained by government forces two days later as he attempted to cross the border into Honduras, but only after having already transmitted his graphic images back to the Washington Post. No one seriously believed the amateurishly absurd Sandinista story that the photog had then committed suicide by seizing a pistol from one of his captors and shooting himself in the side of his head.

It had been the new commander at U.S. Southern Command who only two weeks ago had proposed to Mondale the option of taking down both hostile governments simultaneously. While the Panamanians might be reasonably expected to anticipate imminent military action, General Schwarzkopf had correctly pointed out that the Nicaraguans would likely be caught off guard, lulled into thinking that the-impossible-to-hide rapid American force buildup in the region was aimed solely at their more overtly bellicose neighbor to the south.

"Stormin' Norman" had been brilliantly right. With fewer than 60,000 troops – 25,000 for Panama and about 35,000 for Nicaragua – it had taken less than 72 hours to liberate both countries. Noriega was now dead, having been gunned down by American rangers when he resisted apprehension in Panama City near the Papal Nuncio, where he apparently intended to seek refuge. Ortega was in custody in Managua, and would likely soon face justice at the hands of the newly installed pro-Contra, pro-American, anti-Communist government.

American combined casualties in both theaters had been less than 400 dead, the majority falling in Nicaragua where the U.S. had not had the advantage of pre-existing military bases like it had in Panama. Four hundred was a high cost, Mondale sadly reflected, but probably acceptable given the great good that had been achieved in so short a time.

Mondale reflected with considerable satisfaction the dramatic shift in the balance of political power in the region over the past year. With the savagely successful uprising and coup of last summer (and the CIA had not left any fingerprints) that had overthrown the Grenada communists and meted out the same deadly fate to its leader Bernard Coard as he had to his predecessor six years earlier, Castro's influence was now effectively rolled back to within his own borders. The Caribbean Basin was, for all intents and purposes, once again an American lake.

The President noticed that CNN was finally cutting to the Schwarzkopf press conference in Panama, and turned the sound back on so he could listen. He watched as the burly general in his green jungle-camouflaged battle dress uniform commanded the attention of the assembled reporters and captivated those watching on TV with his colorful, no-nonsense descriptions of the operations and force movements that had led to quick and spectacular victory in both countries.

Good man, thought the President, *he might even be a pretty good VP candidate someday*. Mondale wondered for a moment whether Schwarzkopf was a Republican or Democrat.

Regardless of which party the four-star general belonged to, Mondale knew he owed Schwarzkopf one very large debt.

Critics of the Administration's defense policies, most but not exclusively from the other side of the aisle, had venomously complained for several years that the necessary defense drawdown over which he had so carefully presided had, in fact, eviscerated American military power to an unacceptable degree.

Mondale had always sincerely believed that criticism was baseless. Schwarzkopf's stunning victory over two opponents at once had just proved beyond the shadow of a doubt that the President's critics were as wrong as wrong could be.

Hitting the mute button again, Mondale turned with some considerable satisfaction to the several files on his desk that silently awaited his review, action, or signature.

CHAPTER 14

Managua, Nicaragua

1530 hours, 23 December 1989

Ordinarily Kuhn wouldn't have been on this trip – under most circumstances his boss Colonel Fillman would have been the JAG to deploy with Lieutenant General Mick Casey when the three-star moved his flag from Bergstrom down to the U.S. Southern Command headquarters at Quarry Heights, Panama at the beginning of Operation Just Cause.

Fortunately for Kuhn, his JAG boss was on a three-week Mediterranean cruise, a combination Christmas present/25th Anniversary gift from Col Fillman to his wife. Because of an almost compulsive concern to avoid any possible compromise of operational security prior to commencement of hostilities, General Casey had decided not to recall his staff judge advocate from vacation, and instead had taken his Deputy SJA with him when he went to war. That was just fine with Jack.

Dual hatted as the COMAFOR for United States Southern Command, General Casey was in charge of all of Norm Schwarzkopf's fixed wing air assets for the invasion of Panama and Nicaragua. As with most modern warfare, airpower was the lead element, and his mission was straightforward if deceptively difficult. Casey's job was "simply" to take total control of the skies. To do that, he had to neutralize all enemy air defenses (if the intel was right, mostly relatively old surface-to-air missile systems and their supporting radars), eliminate the ability of either the Panamanian or Nicaraguan Air Forces to launch opposing aircraft, and to substantially degrade the command and control of both enemy armed forces – all within a few hours of the commencement of hostilities.

Casey had achieved all three objectives by masterfully orchestrating an incredibly complex air battle plan that included F-15s and F-16s from several stateside wings, F-111 electronic jamming aircraft, and the coming-out party of the F-117 stealth fighter from Holloman AFB, New Mexico.

The Panamanian Air Force was negated without ever getting a bird airborne, and its defensive radars were destroyed as quickly as they were turned on. Nicaragua at least had gotten several of its aging MIG 21s airborne, but those were mercilessly blotted out in no time by F-16s flying combat air patrol while the F-117s dropped their munitions.

As JAG, one of Kuhn's principal jobs was to make sure that the air battle plan complied with the law of armed conflict, both when it was initially built during the days leading up to the war and as it evolved during combat. He reviewed innumerable bombing targets as they were added to each Air Tasking Order, scrutinizing overhead imagery with the intel guys to make sure no structures like churches or hospitals, protected under the Geneva Conventions, were damaged. In one case, he had recommended a different angle of attack and use of a smaller munition to take out a communications building in Managua so that a nearby museum would be less likely to suffer collateral damage.

Kuhn's portfolio of combat duties during the last week had been extensive and exhausting. He had painstakingly reviewed several sets of SPINS (special instructions) supplementing the broader ROE (rules of engagement) that told the pilots how to fight this particular war. He'd helped Schwarzkopf's Army JAG put the final touches on the enemy POW plan. At Casey's request, Kuhn had stayed up all night with the Public Affairs Officer to help work up likely Q's and A's for the three-star to prep him for CINCSOUTH's press conference. (As it turned out, probably not surprisingly, Schwarzkopf had thoroughly dominated the televised media event with a *tour-de-force* performance and Casey had only been called upon to play a bit part.) Finally, the JAG had repeatedly produced real-time answers to literally dozens of other "off the wall" legal and quasi-legal questions that spewed forth with regularity from the war planners and "targeteers" in the run-up to the war and during its initial stages.

For all intents and purposes, the air war was over barely 30 hours after it started, though Marine Harriers and Army Apache and Blackhawk helicopters continued to provide close air support to the American ground-pounders as they secured the last of their assigned objectives. After the third and essentially final day of combat operations, Kuhn had finally really slept for the first time in a week. He'd gotten fourteen hours of coma-quality slumber on the couch in the two-person Visiting Officers Quarters room at Quarry Heights he shared with five other majors and lieutenant colonels who had deployed along with him.

The past couple of days had been, by comparison, remarkably boring for the JAG, devoid of the incredible intensity that had been so pervasive and palpable while active operations had been underway. Kuhn had thus been flattered and delighted when he got the call this morning from Casey's aide asking if he wanted to accompany the boss on a quick day trip up to Managua, where the three-star intended to personally look in on the F-16 squadron from Luke AFB that had just taken up temporary residence at the Managua International Airport. Casey also was scheduled for a call at the Embassy with the American ambassador to Nicaragua, the aide had told Jack. They'd all be back to Quarry before dark.

Casey and his party had left Quarry Heights late this morning for the short drive to Howard Air Force Base. There were a lot of Panamanians on the streets, Kuhn had noted, for a city that had just been invaded and occupied. Many of the Panamanians had smiled, waved, and given the thumbs up gesture at the four-vehicle convoy as it sped by, appearing genuinely pleased and grateful to be rid of

Noriega and his drug-running thugs. Jack even noticed a street vendor doing a brisk business selling small American flags and tee shirts that had "Gracias America!" emblazoned across the front. *Liberation is a wonderful business*, Jack thought to himself as the convoy entered the Howard main gate to the salutes of the several M-16 carrying security police sentries.

Two minutes later they pulled up on the flightline side of the base operations building, met and saluted by the Howard wing commander, fast-burner Colonel Trip Lanford, and several of his staff. While Casey chatted briefly with Lanford, Jack and the others in the traveling party hustled onto the shiny C-21 military Lear jet that would be their transportation for the short trip north this day. As the two most junior passengers, Jack and Casey's aide, Captain "Jimbo" Evans, hunched down and quickly moved to the two "cheap seats" at the back of the craft. The other two pax were Colonel Charlie Busby, Twelfth Air Force Director of Operations, and Colonel Rob Dolph, the Director of Intelligence for Casey. The colonels took the two front seats in the six-person passenger cabin, leaving the middle left seat for Casey, and the middle right seat for his briefcase.

General Casey had boarded a minute later, and they were airborne four minutes after that.

The trip northwest to Managua was only about five hundred miles, and the C-21 had landed at Augusto Cesar Sadino International Airport just east of Managua just over an hour and a half later.

Security seemed a good deal tighter here, and some of the many American soldiers he saw occupying the airport seemed to Jack to have the proverbial thousand-foot stare – they looked like they'd just been through the ringer. In fact they had, Jack thought, remembering that nearly 90 American rangers had been killed taking this airport just a few days earlier, more than in any other engagement in the short but bloody operation to oust the Sandinistas.

The airport was still closed to commercial traffic. In the place of the airliners that would normally occupy the tarmac, Jack noticed several C-130 and C-141 transports, the F-16s which had just arrived, and even a C-9 Nightingale aeromedical evacuation bird from Scott AFB in Illinois.

They'd been driven a few hundred meters to a small group of hangers where a lieutenant colonel in a flight suit, the commander of the squadron of F-16's who'd just taken up residence at Sadino Airport, waited to greet them. The visit lasted only about fifteen minutes. While General Casey performed a standard "grip and grin" with virtually every member of the flying squadron, Colonels Busby and Dolph went off with the flying squadron ops officer, and Jack sought out the deployed JAG, a captain named Carpenter.

Finding her, Kuhn introduced himself, asked about the C-130 flight the JAG had taken to get down here from Phoenix, and queried whether Carpenter had encountered any serious legal issues or problems since arriving two days earlier. After a brief conversation satisfied him that the young captain had her stuff straight, he left her a handwritten card with his name, office phone number, and the command post number where he could be reached during those few hours during the day when he was not on duty. A moment later, Casey's aide made eye contact with him and gave a nod, the signal that the boss was just about through, and it was time for the "horse-holders" in the traveling party to get back to the cars.

The drive from the airport to the embassy was about fifteen miles, and involved a slightly larger convoy than they had taken on the short jaunt from Quarry Heights to Howard. The general and his aide were driven in the embassy's heavily armored Mercedes while Jack and the two full colonels in his party were driven in a stock Crown Victoria. Three other vehicles – Humvees in the front and the back of the line, and another Crown Vic in the middle – carried Army troops and security personnel from the Air Force OSI.

As the convoy entered Managua proper, Kuhn was struck by the fact that far fewer locals, and far more armed American soldiers and marines, seemed to be on the street than had been the case in Panama City a couple of hours earlier. Further, not all of the Nicaraguans who were out and about, most especially the men, looked like Jack thought people who had just been liberated ought to look. Rather, their stoic stares seemed to Kuhn to contain both hatred and humiliation in roughly equal doses. Well, he rationalized, they'll probably come around after the shock of an unexpected invasion wears off and they begin to understand how much better off they are with the Sandinistas gone.

The visit to the American Embassy took less than an hour – Jack and the others had spent a short amount of time in the Ambassador's office before everyone other than General Casey was politely excused. Colonel Dolph broke away for a little while to meet with some of the CIA spooks stationed there. Kuhn and Colonel Busby killed a few minutes chatting with the Air Force attaché assigned to the Managua station and drinking some of his coffee, while aide Evans waited dutifully for his boss just outside the closed door of the Ambassador's office.

After the boss was done and the traveling party reassembled, Jack, Dolph, and Busby got back into the Crown Vic for their return trip to Sandino Airport. Jack reminded himself that he needed to make sure to get a picture for Margie of Lago Xolotlan just to the north of Managua. The best spot, he remembered, should be right after they turned off Bolivar Drive onto the Pan-American Highway, a place where the lake was just a couple hundred yards north of the road. Given his preoccupation with people-watching on the way into town, he knew he had missed his next to last opportunity to snap a picture of the huge and beautiful lake.

As the convoy made the turn onto the major thoroughfare, Jack pulled his small 35 mm camera out of his briefcase and began to peer through the viewing port to line up his photo.

Looking left at the lake, Kuhn never saw the truck that barreled in from a side street on the other side of the highway and broadsided the armored Mercedes in which General Casey and his aide were riding two vehicles ahead. As the driver of Kuhn's Crown Victoria slammed on his brakes and swerved right to avoid the melee, Kuhn's forehead slammed into the window of the left rear door through which he had been trying to focus his camera.

Dazed by the head blow, Kuhn was at first only vaguely aware of shots being fired. "Get down!" the OSI agent driving their car yelled at his three passengers. As Jack fought sluggishly to comply, he noticed the almost ticklish sensation of warm blood streaming down his face and then felt a paralyzingly sharp pain in his left shoulder – he intuited from the experience of a similar pain he had felt a long time ago after getting creamed in a high school football game that his collarbone had probably been broken. As he crouched down, he noticed that Busby was doing the same in the front passenger seat, but that Colonel Dolph, apparently stunned by whatever he'd bumped into, was still sitting upright next to him. Without thinking, Jack reflexively reached up with his right arm, grabbed the front of Dolph's uniform shirt, and tugged through the pain to pull the colonel's torso and head down below the level of the back window.

Although Jack couldn't see what was happening from his hunkered down posture, a second later a bullet fired from behind penetrated and explosively shattered the rear window. The driver instantly threw the vehicle into reverse and floored it, slamming his semi-prone passengers forward into the backside of the seat ahead of them. Almost immediately, Kuhn felt the backward accelerating vehicle strike something – make that someone, he thought – hard. Fighting hard to maintain his consciousness through the throbbing pain in his head and shoulder, he heard several more shots ring out behind the vehicle, followed by a good deal of shouting. Then things got quiet. Just before he passed out, he allowed himself to think that he might just live through all this . . .

Jack woke up with a hangover-quality headache to the insistently loud drone of aircraft engines. It took him several seconds to realize that he was strapped to a bed of some sort inside of an airplane. As he struggled to put together the pieces, he noticed that a tube extended into his right forearm from a clear bag hanging next to where he lay.

Seeing that Kuhn had opened his eyes, a female lieutenant in a green flight suit walked over to his bed and looked down at him. "You still with us, sir?" she asked.

"I think so," replied Kuhn groggily. "Where am I?"

"You're in the back end of a C-9 over the Gulf of Mexico about 500 miles south of San Antonio," came the reply from the concerned face above him. It took Jack a couple of seconds to figure out she was a flight nurse.

"How badly banged up am I," asked Kuhn, now starting to remember the chaos that had preceded his unconsciousness.

"I've seen worse," the lieutenant answered. "You've got a pretty good gash on your forehead, you probably have a concussion, and it looks like your shoulder is broken. The good news is that you'll live," she smiled down at him.

"We going to Wilford Hall?" he asked, referring to the Air Force's big hospital at Lackland Air Force Base in San Antonio.

"You got it," she replied, "there's a bed with your name on it waiting there."

"How about the boss?" Kuhn queried, just a bit ashamed he'd appeared so exclusively interested in his own situation.

"I'm OK, Jack," came the voice of the three-star from somewhere behind him.

"Hey sir, good to hear your voice," Jack slowly stammered back.

"The general has a pretty loose definition of what OK means," the nurse interjected.

"The docs say my right leg is broken in a couple places, but otherwise I'm OK," the general corrected. "That Mercedes is tough as a tank."

"How about the others?" Kuhn asked.

"Everybody's going to make it, Jack," replied Casey. "Rob's got a concussion like you – he's in la-la land right now in the bunk behind me. Jimbo just got a few scrapes – I think he's up front trying to talk the flight crew into giving him some stick time before we land."

"And Charlie?" asked Kuhn.

"Not a scratch. I sent that slacker back to Quarry to mind the store until Pete can get down there and provide some adult supervision," answered the general. "Pete" referred to Casey's vice commander, Major General Peter Gavigan, who had remained behind at Bergstrom when the war started, but was now probably already in the air heading south to backfill Casey.

"The security guys?" asked Kuhn, remembering the soldiers and OSI agents who undoubtedly had helped save all their lives.

"Think only one Army guy got hurt bad. Somebody told me they were taking him directly to a hospital in Managua for some surgery that couldn't wait," answered Casey. "We'll keep our fingers crossed for him."

"Amen," replied Jack, suddenly wincing in pain as he attempted to move his head.

"That button by your right hand will give you a shot of morphine whenever you need it," offered the nurse, "and you look like you might just need it."

"Good medical advice," added General Casey, "I've used my own button a few times already."

Always good to obey one's superiors, thought Jack as he reached for the button and gave it a long hard push.

Almost instantly, he felt a numbing warmness ooze through his body, and his pain subsided. "See you on the ground, tiger" he heard someone say in the distance as he willingly surrendered to the morphine and fell back to a welcome drug-induced slumber.

CHAPTER 15

The Pentagon
Arlington, Virginia
0700 hours, 3 August 1990

"Iraq Invades Kuwait," or a close variant thereof, was the banner headline of each of the several newspapers that lay on a coffee table in the anteroom to the "tank," the Pentagon's mother of all secure conference rooms. The stories beneath those headlines all described how, after several weeks of escalating tension over a border dispute, the forces of Saddam Hussein had yesterday steam-rolled its tiny but oil-rich neighbor to the south in a classic blitzkrieg military movement. The Kuwait head of state, Emir Sheikh Jabber al-Ahmed al-Sabah, had narrowly escaped to Saudi Arabia – his brother Sheikh Fahd was much less fortunate, having been shot and killed in the family's Kuwait City palace when Iraqi special operations forces had stormed it.

Inside the tank was a very small group of American's most important military decision-makers. Sam Nunn, the Secretary of Defense for the past two years and his youngish one-star military assistant were joined by Army General Colin Powell (appointed by President Mondale less a year earlier to be the next Chairman of the Joint Chiefs of Staff) and the four-star heads of the Army, Navy, Air Force and Marines. The usual entourage of aides, deputies, and assistants were noticeably absent, having been specifically dis-invited to this particular meeting.

At the briefing podium was a haggard-looking Navy captain giving the intelligence update – the officer clearly had not slept much in the last 24 hours, but neither had the men who were now listening to him.

He pointed to a briefing screen that showed overhead imagery with "1430Z, 1 August 1990" stamped in small yellow letters in the lower right corner of the slide. "This is how the Iraqi forces were arrayed just prior to commencement of operations," the captain spoke. "Although this picture unmistakably shows an offensive force postured to move forward, CIA assessments during the buildup over the past two weeks have consistently concluded that the Iraqis were unlikely to attack and were instead saber rattling in a show of force, presumably to leverage upcoming negotiations with the Kuwaitis. As you know, that assessment on the part of the CIA didn't change until about 36 hours ago."

The briefer then displayed a series of overhead pictures and maps with various military symbols, carefully explaining to the Secretary and JCS the sequence of events. He described how the Iraqis had attacked using their very best, elite Republican Guard (RG) units as well as highly trained Special Forces teams. A Republican Guard mechanized armor division, he explained, had headed south to Al Jahrah on the Gulf of Kuwait after crossing the border, then turned east to envelop Kuwait City itself. Meanwhile, Iraqi special forces had worked from the inside out, having entered Kuwait City by air and sea to seize key government facilities such as ministries, the TV station, and the Emir's palace. At the same time, another RG armored division quickly worked its deadly way through the southern portion of Kuwait to neutralize any remaining Kuwaiti soldiers and seize the International Airport as well as the emirate's only two military airfields, at Al Jaber and Ali al Salem.

It had been as one-sided as a military operation can be, and the entire operation, pointed out the captain in reluctant admiration, took less than twelve hours. The Iraqi army was unquestionably in total control of Kuwait and Saddam was now pouring in huge numbers of reinforcements from their staging areas in southern Iraq. Disturbingly, said the captain, Iraqi tanks were also now taking up positions in defensive revetments being dug along the border between Kuwait and Saudi Arabia.

"Good briefing, Captain, thank you," muttered Nunn, "you're dismissed." The captain hastily exited.

"O.K. gentlemen," began SecDef, "Colin and I have a meeting with the President across the river in three hours. What can I tell him about options."

It was Powell who responded. "The military options are going to be pretty limited, Mr. Secretary. For starters, we have very few forces presently in the region, and not all that many left in Europe that could move relatively easily to the region. If Saddam had done this three or four years ago, we might have had more flexibility. Today, however, I'm just not sure that our available force structure would credibly support offensive operations to eject Iraq from Kuwait, at least not without unacceptable numbers of American casualties."

"How many troops would you need to go on offense?" asked Nunn.

"I wouldn't be comfortable with much less than half a million," responded Powell. The Army's four-star chief nodded in clear agreement with the Chairman.

Nunn immediately understood the problem. With the large-scale military reductions that had taken place over the past five years, it was unlikely that the Army and Marines could muster even a quarter million combat ready troops in the short time frame they were talking about. In fact, although inferior in its weapons and technology, Saddam's army was now the world's third largest (behind only the Chinese and the Soviets) and three times as large as its American counterpart.

"You mentioned casualties. Assuming we could only muster half that number, what kind of KIA numbers do you envision if we took the offensive?" asked Nunn.

"You know how strongly I feel that if we go in anywhere, we must go in with overwhelmingly superior force. If we don't, I think we're talking potentially in the range of ten to fifteen thousand American dead, maybe more if he goes chemical or biological," said Powell. He segued directly into his continuing analysis.

"Secondly, if we just want to play defense and insert U.S. forces into Saudi Arabia purely to protect the Kingdom and its oilfields, which I think we *could* do with something less than that quarter million force you just described, we've still got some serious problems."

"Such as?" shot back Nunn.

"Such as the formidable logistical difficulty TRANSCOM will face getting that force in place, particularly if the West Germans don't play ball."

That one made Nunn stop and think. The West Germans were now actively involved in very serious and delicate reunification discussions with the East German government, with the tacit but clear approval of the Soviet Union. If the Soviets vigorously opposed American military action in Iraq, which they were certain to do, it wasn't farfetched at all to think the West Germans might decide it wasn't in their own self-interest to allow a huge American force to transit Rhein Main hub on their way to the Middle East. Not if they wanted the Soviets to agree to let the wall come down. And there was, Nunn knew, no reasonable alternative to using the German base as a stopover to the desert.

Powell continued, "There's also the problem of the Saudis themselves. If we're only capable of going there in a defensive mode, I'm not very confident that they'll allow a large foreign military force to enter the Kingdom, especially since we're likely to be there for a very long time. Plus, the Saudis are businessmen at heart. They're used to dealing with Saddam, with all his warts, and may well think they can negotiate some kind of acceptable accommodation with him."

"There are a couple of other things," said Powell. "If Vietnam taught us anything, it's how important it is to have broad support for any American military operation. Maybe the President can muster public support here at home and get Congress on board, but it's iffy in my mind whether such support will last long if hundreds or thousands of body bags start passing through Dover.

"Finally, I'd feel a lot better about a military option if we had approval and help from the rest of the world, or at least a significant portion of it. Frankly, I don't see that happening. The Soviets are sure to veto any U.N. resolution supporting military operations against Iraq, as are the Chinese. The French might too, based on their long-standing business partnership with Iraq.

"Plus, for lots of reasons, the Kuwaitis are not terribly popular with their neighbors – they're pretty much regarded by the other countries in the region as selfish, rude, and snooty. So I doubt that anybody in the neighborhood will be willing to stick their neck out with troops or money to help get Kuwait out from under Saddam's thumb, at least not without more arm-twisting than I think the President is prepared to do."

"How about Syria?" asked Nunn.

"Syria can't like what's happening one bit, but I suspect Assad will get sufficient assurances from the Soviets that his country is not at any risk from Iraq. I'm guessing that, along with some amount of rubles, will satisfy him."

Damn, thought Nunn, *this might be a lot easier if Gorbachev didn't have so many good cards in his hand right now.* And, it suddenly struck him, *they're going to have even more good cards if we can't do anything about this.*

"At the bottom line, Mr. Secretary," Powell concluded, "I don't think we have much in the way of viable military options to offer the President, at least not in the short to mid-term. I think our approach is going to have to be diplomatic only."

"Do the rest of you agree?" said Nunn, looking in turn at the Army and Air Force Chiefs of Staff, the Navy CNO, and the Commandant of the Marine Corps.

Each nodded joyless assent.

"Then it's probably not going to be a fun meeting with the President," Nunn correctly concluded.

CHAPTER 16

Riyadh, Kingdom of Saudi Arabia
1130, 17 Jumada I, 1412 (Islamic Calendar)
(November 24, 1991)

It had been a treacherously winding road that led to this day and place, metaphorically thought King Fahd bin Abdul Aziz Al Saud of Saudi Arabia, remembering back sixteen months earlier when the Iraqi army had steam-rolled their way through Kuwait to the Saudi border.

Saddam had surprised him, and the rest of the Arab world, by making good on his blustering and bellicose threats against his tiny but rich neighbor to the south. By doing so, Saddam had radically altered the correlation of forces in the region and dramatically improved his own military position and political influence, albeit at the cost of a good deal of world condemnation as well as a high sounding (but hopelessly porous, the King knew) arms embargo mandated by the United Nations.

Three days after the invasion, Fahd had, upon the recommendation of Prince Bandar, the Kingdom's young ambassador to Washington, secretly received representatives of the American president here in Riyadh. Secretary Nunn and General Powell had offered him the protection of their armed forces, proposing to place nearly 100,000 American troops and a significant number of combat aircraft in the Kingdom, ostensibly to deter Saddam from moving into Saudi Arabia from his newly acquired stronghold in Kuwait.

Had he accepted the American proposal, Fahd knew, he would undoubtedly not now be preparing to host the comprehensive peace settlement ceremony that would take place here in his principal palace less than an hour from now.

It had been a complex calculus, he remembered, one without a clear answer. While an American presence of that size would likely have deterred an Iraqi thrust into the Kingdom's precious oilfields in the northeastern quarter of the country, Nunn had admitted that it would take at least two months – and maybe a bit longer – to put a significant portion of that defensive force in place, during which time the Kingdom would have been extraordinarily vulnerable, at least from a purely military point of view.

More importantly, Nunn and Powell had equivocated when Crown Prince Abdallah, Fahd's half-brother who had commanded the Saudi National Guard since the early 60s, had asked if the Americans were prepared to commit the significantly larger number of forces that would be necessary to forcibly move the Iraqi army out of Kuwait if diplomacy ultimately failed and such military action should become necessary to protect the Kingdom's security.

That equivocation posed a dilemma for Fahd. Although Saudi Arabia had long allowed a small cadre of American military advisors to assist the Kingdom's National Guard and the Royal Saudi Air Force, it had never in its history allowed any significant foreign military force to be garrisoned inside its borders.

He knew that any long-term presence of non-Muslim military forces would cause him no end of trouble with many of his own people, who would accuse him of breaching his solemn duty as "Custodian of the Two Holy Mosques" by allowing a powerful force of "infidels" inside the very Kingdom where Islam was born. The fact that the American army now included Sodomites would only exacerbate that resentment, Fahd knew, particularly among the sizable fundamentalist element in his country.

He also was sure that the presence of a sizable American force in Saudi Arabia would make any diplomatic solution to the Kuwait crisis infinitely more unlikely. Saddam, like almost all leaders in this region, was obsessed with the concepts of honor and face. He'd likely find it impossible to give any diplomatic ground if he thought such action would be perceived by many in the Arab world as flinching in the face of American military power.

No, Fahd remembered thinking at the time, the American proposal would only lead to diplomatic stalemate, and require the indefinite presence of American forces in the Kingdom. That was simply unacceptable.

Yet, Iraq's forces were still positioned like a dagger prepared to stab into the Kingdom's oil rich jugular at the whim of the Iraqi leader. That was equally unacceptable.

It had been the Soviets who provided the solution to his dilemma.

Eduord Shevardnadze and his remarkable young assistant Putin had called on the King two days later, carrying with them a dramatically different proposal. If Saudi Arabia would decline the American offer, they had told him, the USSR would guarantee the Kingdom's safety and sovereignty not with a massive infusion of troops, but rather by calling upon their long-standing relationship with Saddam. Shevardnadze had proposed putting a very small force, less than 1,500 troops, between Dhahran and the Kuwait border in a mostly symbolic "peacekeeping" role. Given the historically close relationship between the Iraqis and the USSR - particularly Iraq's continuing dependence on Soviet arms, equipment, and advisors, young Putin had explained – placement of such a force on Saudi soil would ensure with certainly that Saddam would not move on the Kingdom.

The Russian foreign minister had further pledged to the King that the Soviet Union would devote whatever resources were necessary to broker and ensure a just settlement to the Kuwait matter, and that such settlement would include the withdrawal of Iraqi troops, first from the Saudi border and then from Kuwait itself. Shevardnadze told the King that achieving such a resolution would take no more than a year, and probably less time than that.

Finally, he assured the King, as soon as the peace had been brokered, the small Soviet force would go home.

The King had then excused himself to consider his options. It was not an easy thing to trust the Soviets – the godlessness of their communist theology and their long history of territorial ambition weighed heavily on the King's mind.

Yet based on what he had observed of Gorbachev over the past several years, Fahd had the feeling that he could be trusted. The Soviet premier had been the architect, after all, of an unprecedented *glasnost* in his country, his economic reforms had begun to significantly resuscitate his country's once-faltering economy, and he had made good on his remarkable promise to the world to dramatically reduce nuclear stockpiles. Crown Prince Abdallah agreed with his monarch's logic, and the decision was made.

The Soviets had been nearly as good as their word. Saddam had not moved on the Kingdom, and although it had taken somewhat longer than the year the Shevardnadze had promised, the USSR-brokered resolution was now at hand.

In exchange for a favorable border adjustment of several kilometers and substantial Kuwaiti monetary reparations for oil the small nation would now admit to having "slant drilled" from Iraqi territory, Iraq would formally acknowledge Kuwait's sovereignty and conduct a phased withdrawal of its troops over the next two years. The first phase of the withdrawal would begin immediately after the agreement was signed and result in the removal all Iraqi offensive forces within ten kilometers of the Saudi border.

During the two-year transition period, the Kuwait Royal House would not be restored to power. Rather, as the Iraq military withdrawal was nearing completion, a plebiscite would be supervised by four members of the Arab league – Egypt, Saudi Arabia, Syria, and Jordan – to determine whether the Kuwaiti people wanted the Royals to return.

Finally, the United Nations-imposed economic sanctions and arms embargo imposed upon Iraq since shortly after the invasion would be lifted incrementally as the Iraqis met the various withdrawal phase points specified in the agreement.

It was far from a perfect solution, Fahd knew, but it *was* a viable solution. Saddam would continue to be dangerous, since his huge army – particularly his deadly efficient Republican Guard tank divisions – would be intact, undamaged, and available for any future adventures he might have in mind. The world was betting a lot on the promise and hope that the Soviets could henceforth keep him in line.

Allah willing, the treaty might just allow a return to near normalcy on the Arabian Peninsula. King Fahd certainly hoped so.

CHAPTER 17

The Pentagon
Arlington, Virginia
0645 hours, 2 October 1992

As he walked robotically down the escalator from the mega-bus stop next to the five-sided colossus, it occurred to Lieutenant Colonel Jack Kuhn that he'd been lucky to avoid a DC assignment as long as he had. Compared to any place else he'd lived in his 42 years on the planet, Kuhn thought as he moved with the rest of the herd coming to work this morning, this town unquestionably was the least "user-friendly."

For starters, it was obscenely expensive. When they were getting ready to move here from Texas last summer, Jack and Margie had choked on the asking prices for homes anywhere within a thirty-mile distance of the nation's capital. Neither of them could imagine spending the $400,000 or so that sellers were asking (and apparently getting!) for a basic four bedroom two thousand square foot home in northern Virginia. Even if they were lucky enough to qualify for a mortgage, with the current interest rate of just under 10%, their monthly payments would have been over $3,500 per month, or roughly two thirds of a lieutenant colonel's take home pay.

They'd gotten a break of sorts when they were able to find a three-bedroom townhouse in Burke to rent. The owner, a JAG colonel who was being reassigned to Nebraska, had not gouged them, and they'd signed a two-year lease for $2,100 a month. It was much smaller and more cramped for the four of them than the base house they'd had in Texas, but it was more affordable than anything else they'd seen.

Just as importantly, it got the Kuhns in a good public school district – Heather and Cindy were able to attend the very large (over three thousand students) but very good Lake Braddock High School. Both girls continued to do well in school, which meant, Jack shuddered, that an additional line item of "tuition & college expenses" would be inserted into their already tight family budget next year when Heather graduated from high school.

Getting to and from the Pentagon was as depressing a daily exercise as anything he'd ever experienced. Because he was just a lieutenant colonel, he was not nearly high enough on the DoD totem pole to qualify for a parking pass anywhere near the building. That had been just as well, he knew, since the Iraq-Kuwait stalemate had sent the price of gas skyrocketing to over two dollars a gallon. Jack opted instead for public transportation.

Every workday morning, he dragged himself out of bed at 5 a.m. in order to leave the house by 5:30 to drive the beat-up old Gremlin he'd bought to the Rolling Valley Metro parking lot. There he'd get in a line with a lot of other early birds to board the 5:50 a.m. Metrobus which then headed east down Old Keene Mill Road. The bus made a dozen stops over seven miles before it headed north along I-95 for ten miles or so to the Pentagon. On those rare good days when there was no rain, snow, or accident anywhere along the route, the trip took around 45 minutes. On the far more frequent bad days, the trip could take anywhere between an hour and pick a number.

His trip home from the Pentagon, usually around 6:30 p.m., was almost always even more of a hassle, mostly because about half the time there'd be no seats left by the time he got on the bus. That left him standing to be continually jostled in the crowded aisle for most of the trip back to Burke – by the time he got home around 7:30 or 8, his feet and back were sore, his uniform shirt frequently sweat-stained, and Margie and the girls had usually already eaten supper.

He decided he'd better quit fretting about things he couldn't do anything about. Reaching the bottom of the escalator, he and the herd from his bus walked about a hundred feet, turned right, and got on an even longer up escalator that led to the Pentagon concourse. When he got near the top, Jack pulled his building pass out of his wallet to have it ready to show the GSA security guard standing watch as the stream of humanity filed in for another Pentagon day. Jack walked through the concourse, trundled up the long marble ramp to the third floor, took a right into Corridor 10, turned into the stairwell a hundred feet later near the C ring, walked up one flight, turned left when he entered the fourth floor, then another left when he reached the E ring, and walked the final fifty feet to the door marked SAF/IGS.

He didn't really have an office – few lieutenant colonels did in this Building. Rather, he had a cramped modular cubicle – there were twelve such cubicles in the ten by thirty foot office occupied by the Senior Officer Inquiry Division of the Office of the Air Force Inspector General.

Kuhn was one of three full-time legal advisors who worked with the cadre of Air Force officers whose job was to conduct investigations into allegations of wrongdoing on the part of senior colonels and generals. Kuhn had never been as frustrated by any assignment so much as this one.

Much of that frustration stemmed from the way senior officer investigations were conducted. As an Air Force lawyer, he had always taken pride in the fact that the military legal system in which he worked was incredibly fair and even-handed, affording full due process for those accused of infractions and insisting on stringent safeguards for truth. For example, Jack knew from his own extensive personal experience that the military court-martial process, despite popular misconceptions to the contrary, afforded all defendants every right given in a civilian criminal trial, and some additional rights as well.

The area of IG investigations, he had discovered, was one in which those noble priorities didn't seem to apply at all – the career officers being investigated, usually on the basis of anonymous complaints, were afforded virtually no rights. They frequently were not fully advised of the allegations against them until they were just about to testify (always at the very end of the investigation) and in many cases weren't even allowed to have their attorney present when they were questioned by the investigating officer. Subjects were never told who the witnesses against them were. Further, those witnesses testified secretly and unaccountably, never subjected to the kind of meaningful cross-examination that was so vital, in Kuhn's view, to verify truthfulness. And, if as frequently happened, the investigator happened to conclude that the senior officer was "guilty" by the inexcusably minimal "preponderance of the evidence" standard of proof the IG used, the unlucky subject – his or her career now irrevocably in the toilet – would still never be allowed to see the unredacted evidence upon which that verdict was based.

This incredibly shoddy system was exacerbated, in Jack's view, by the kinds of officers who were selected to become investigators. They were all full colonels who, by and large, were former wing commanders who had NOT been selected for promotion to flag rank. The Inspector General himself, a lieutenant general named Kadish who Jack thought had likely been chosen for this three-star billet as a reward for long and faithful service rather than for any particular aptitude, thought that the fact his investigators were no longer competitive for further promotion contributed to their independence. From Jack's perspective – somewhat closer to ground truth he thought than General Kadish – it looked rather different. Many of the investigators he worked with seemed to carry a fairly sizable chip on their shoulders based on their non-selection for flag promotion, and seemed awfully eager to find official fault with those who *had* gotten promoted to general officer rank.

At the bottom line, based on a year's worth of work with the IG, Jack estimated that IG "findings and conclusions" actually got it right – or at least landed in the general neighborhood of the truth – less than two thirds of the time. It was an abominable system, Jack thought bitterly, one he was embarrassed and frustrated to be a part of.

One recent case had pushed him over the edge. The IG had investigated an anonymous complaint, clearly from somebody with an ax to grind, about a wing commander who had just been selected for promotion to brigadier general. His alleged "crime" had been signing a performance report on a subordinate that contained an incorrect duty title for the ratee. Despite the unequivocal evidence that the commander had signed the report on the advice of his personnel experts, the IG investigator had nevertheless concluded he was guilty of making a "false official statement." And although the unlucky commander's boss had thereafter reviewed the IG's findings and rightly found them utterly incongruous and legally insufficient, the wing commander was nevertheless still red-lined – taken off the promotion list – after Senate Armed Services Committee staffers read the IG's stridently worded summary report and advised the Pentagon that the SASC would not confirm him to be a brigadier general.

That case and several others like it had convinced Jack of the need to try to do something about the system. He'd spent a lot of evenings and weekends of late working up a lengthy and detailed memorandum on the need for reform, including several examples and a number of specific suggestions on how the system could be easily improved. It was, in Jack's view, a very good piece of legal analysis, and he'd sent it last week to the Judge Advocate General of the Air Force for his consideration.

Sitting down in his cubicle this morning, he noticed a yellow phone message in the middle of the counter that passed for his desk. *Rita called - Brig Gen Buckingham wants to talk to you re: your memo at 0800 – his office*, the handwritten note said.

Jack was elated. Benjamin Buckingham was the one-star Deputy Judge Advocate General (DJAG), the number two ranking military lawyer in the Air Force. Kuhn allowed himself some considerable satisfaction that his memo had gotten the kind of high-level attention he'd intended and hoped for.

About an hour later, he made the short walk down the E-ring to the small suite that was the Pentagon home of Major General Andy Elliott, the Judge Advocate General, his deputy Brigadier General Buckingham, and their secretaries and executive officers. Kuhn had met Anita Dettmer, General Buckingham's pleasant German-born secretary, before – she offered him a cup of coffee (which he'd accepted) and told him that the General was running a few minutes late. Jack took a seat in one of the two chairs that served as a waiting area, and picked up the Washington Post from the end table next to him.

The lead story on the front page, not surprisingly, was about the continuing Iraq stalemate, and the upcoming Persian Gulf "peace" talks (really how-to-get-Iraq-out-of-Kuwait talks, Jack knew) being brokered – largely behind the scenes – by the Soviet Union. Those talks were scheduled to begin today in Manama, Bahrain, a small island nation just off the coast of northern Saudi Arabia. The sanctions must finally be starting to hurt Saddam, Jack thought. Either that or Gorbachev must really be applying some big-time pressure to the long-time Soviet client.

The other big story on the front-page covered Vice President Gore's emotional announcement that he would not be a candidate for the presidency in 1992. Kuhn had seen a snippet of the tear-filled press conference on CNN last night before he went to bed. Gore had said that his first duty had to be to his family, and that it would be impossible to carry on a campaign while Tipper was working through her long recuperation from the auto accident that had badly shattered both her legs just last month.

Hard to fault his priorities, Jack opined sympathetically to himself. The thought then crossed Jack's mind that Gore's decision was probably also a smart one politically. With President Mondale's badly slumping approval ratings, with inflation and unemployment again on the rise, and with the growing perception of American impotency in the international arena, it didn't look like any Democrat was going to be able to beat the Republican candidate, whoever that might be, next year. Jack chided himself for his cynicism. *Washington can turn you into a cynic in no time*, he rationalized.

As Kuhn was starting to turn the page, General Buckingham strode in from the E ring hallway.

"Sorry I'm late, Jack," the one-star said, "come on in."

"No problem, sir," answered Kuhn.

"Sit down. I want to talk to you about the memo you wrote," started Buckingham after closing his office door. "It's an impressive piece of legal writing, and you make some valid points, but I think you're missing the big picture."

Jack slumped at the sudden realization that this was clearly not going to be a congratulatory discussion. "I'm all ears, sir."

"Congress demands that the military services aggressively self-police themselves. That's why we have an IG system in the first place, to identify and weed out officers who misuse their positions or authority."

"I don't disagree with that," interjected Jack. "My concern is that the current system doesn't do a very good job of sorting out the guilty from the innocent."

"Do you understand how presumptuous that sounds Jack?" continued Buckingham, "particularly since Congress hasn't given any indication that they're not fully satisfied with our current system. The SASC routinely review reports of investigation generated by the IG – don't you think somebody on the Hill would have squawked by now if they thought our system was flawed?"

"That might be because they don't have a clear enough sight picture to know one way or the other, sir," Kuhn replied, thinking as he said it that he probably sounded as presumptuous as Buckingham thought he was.

"Come on, Jack, give the folks on the Hill a little credit," answered the one star, "they've been around in this town a lot longer than you have."

"I can't disagree with that," answered Jack.

"Good," said Buckingham. "Tell you what I'll do. When TJAG gets back from his trip to the Pacific in a couple of weeks, I'll talk to him about your concerns. Let's give him some time to review the matter and consider the points you make."

"Thank you," replied Kuhn, hoping the insincerity of his "gratitude" wasn't obvious to Buckingham. He harbored no illusions that Buckingham would fairly articulate his concerns, or even actually pass his memo along, to General Elliott.

"Let's talk about you for a minute, Jack," the Deputy TJAG continued. "You've got a big future. You were a great SJA, and you performed magnificently at the pointy end of the spear in Central America. We don't have any other JAG I know who's been awarded both a Bronze Star *and* a Purple Heart. You're a very important role model for other judge advocates."

Jack's mind instantly flashed back to the day in Managua when he'd been hurt in the attack on General Casey's convoy. Five of the six attackers had been killed, and luckily only one American had died, thank God. Jack remembered his weeklong stay at the hospital in San Antonio, and the four weeks he spent at home on convalescent leave while his broken collarbone healed up. The two-inch scar on his forehead just below his hairline was now the only visible reminder of that horrific day.

"Your name came up a couple weeks ago when General Elliott and I were talking to the career management folks about some upcoming assignment vacancies. We think you'd be a very good fit for the CCDC job across the river at Bolling."

That took Jack by surprise. Being a Chief Circuit Defense Counsel was one of the best jobs a lieutenant colonel lawyer could get. He'd be in charge, he knew, of a couple dozen Air Force defense attorneys at bases throughout the eastern part of the United States. There'd be a lot more travel, but also more money in the form of *per diem* entitlements when he was on the road. Most importantly, he thought, CCDCs almost always seemed to get promoted to full colonel, a not insignificant consideration since he'd be meeting the colonel's board in the primary zone within the next two years.

"If that's what you want me to do, I'd be happy to take the job, sir," said Kuhn, meaning it this time.

"Great," answered the one-star. "We're probably gonna need you over there pretty quick. I'll work the details with Col Brasher, but you need to start winding up whatever you're doing at IGS."

"Yes, sir," answered Kuhn.

"Hate to run you out, Jack, but I've got to get ready for my next meeting. Have a good one." Kuhn responded to Buckingham's unambiguous cue and quickly departed his office. He thanked Rita again for the coffee, and headed back down the Pentagon E-ring toward his office.

He knew he'd just been rolled. But he also suspected that was how a lot of things worked in this damn building and this damn town. Marveling at Buckingham's smoothness, it occurred to him that the Deputy TJAG's reputation for "playing it safe" and avoiding controversy at all costs was probably well deserved. Well, thought Jack, there's probably something to be said for the kind of pragmatism that Buckingham was known for – the one-star's career had flourished by his strict adherence to that "don't trouble trouble until trouble troubles you" philosophy. In fact, Jack realized, his experience in the IG shop corroborated that view. Risk-taking by officers, no matter how well intended, seemed frequently to be a one-way street to an investigation and getting one's career thoroughly derailed.

As he got back to his cubicle, though, it suddenly occurred to Jack that there was a very fine line between pragmatism and moral cowardice.

CHAPTER 18

Pentagon City, Virginia
1900 hours, 2 October 1992

Lieutenant Colonel Larry Wilkins sat alone with his draft Guinness in a small booth in the modernish Duffy's Irish pub in Pentagon City, a relatively new hodgepodge collection of modern high-rise office buildings, apartments, retail outlets and restaurants as well as the large Pentagon City Mall located just east of the five-sided building. Duffy's was an incredibly convenient watering hole, since his small apartment was literally three floors above the pub. It also made his commute extraordinarily easy since he was literally one Metro stop away from the Pentagon. His daily sojourn from apartment to office was less than fifteen minutes.

Although Larry frequently used the busy bar as his Friday night hunting ground, he was not in conquest mode this particular evening. Rather, he was reflecting on the implications of the past week.

Wilkins was now the Chief of Officer Assignments in AF/JAEC, the Pentagon office symbol for The JAG Career Management division. It was in many ways the most influential job a JAG lieutenant colonel could have, given that he was responsible for determining where every military lawyer in the grades of captain through lieutenant colonel was assigned, subject of course to approval of The Judge Advocate General. Full colonel assignments were handled by his boss, Colonel Brasher, but given Brasher's frequent absences from the office due to his propensity to maximize his own "official travel" around the world, Larry frequently got to play in the O-6 assignment-making process as well, particularly when it came to obtaining Brigadier General

Buckingham's support of Career Management's assignment recommendations before they went to TJAG for final approval.

Buckingham had been Larry's strongest supporter for the past several years – as a colonel, Buckingham had been head of the Environmental Law Division where Larry had been assigned after his participation in the ASTRA program. A year after Buckingham got his first star and became the head lawyer for Tactical Air Command, he had "drafted" Wilkins to be his head lawyer at Myrtle Beach AFB, South Carolina. Larry's time in that SJA position was shorter than normal, since that base was shuttered by the base closure commission a scant 18 months after Larry's arrival. Larry saw that short tenure as an opportunity, however, since the full colonel's board was likely to view him as a "fast burner" if his follow-on job was sufficiently prestigious. The Chief of Officer Assignments gig filled that bill perfectly. Buckingham, who had recently been nominated to return to Washington as the next DJAG, had successfully lobbied to have Wilkins given the powerful job.

Buckingham and Wilkins' symbiotic mentor-mentee relationship served them both very well. Most importantly from Larry's perspective, it allowed him to significantly strengthen his position visa vis his likely competitors for promotion to general officer several years down the road.

Larry regarded Jack Kuhn as one of his most serious competitors, and perhaps the most dangerous to Larry's ambitious personal career plan. Jack, he knew, was the closest thing to a "war hero" the JAG Corps had, and he had succeeded at every job he'd been given throughout his career thus far. Larry had worked very hard a year earlier to convince Buckingham and TJAG to assign Jack, who had no previous Pentagon experience, as a legal advisor to the Senior Officer Inquiry Division of the Air Force Inspector General. He knew Jack would salute smartly and do a good job, but more importantly from Wilkin's point of view, it was not a job that anybody who really mattered would likely notice at all.

Larry's plan to keep Jack invisible for at least a few years had unraveled a couple weeks back. Buckingham had called Wilkins to his office and told him to find a different job in DC for Kuhn – apparently Jack had written a critical legal memo that Buckingham had considered very insightful, but also very dangerous. Both Buckingham and Elliott were fans of Jack and wanted him to be promoted to colonel next year when he was in the primary zone, so Larry's personal challenge was to find a job for him that was "good enough," but not too good. After a lot of thought, he settled on the Chief Circuit Defense Counsel position for Jack across the river at Bolling AFB. It seemed to fit the bill – although it pretty much ensured Kuhn would make colonel when eligible, more importantly, at least to Larry's way of thinking, no CCDC in the history of the Air Force had ever been later promoted to flag rank.

It was, Larry congratulated himself as he finished the last sip of his beer, the best available option to ensure that Kuhn would not be standing in his way in a few years when they were both senior enough to be considered for promotion to brigadier general.

As he put his glass down, he noticed two attractive women sit down in the next booth over. Maybe, he decided, he should go hunting tonight.

CHAPTER 19

Washington, DC

1730 hours, 5 February 1994

Colonel (Select) Jack Kuhn always enjoyed the view during final approach into Franklin Delano Roosevelt National Airport when the aircraft came in from the south straight up the Potomac River. When he was sitting on the right side of the plane as he was now, he could see Bolling Air Force Base clearly as he descended, including the building that housed his own office, on the opposite side of the river.

He'd flown in and out of FDR a lot over the past twelve months, Jack thought as the 727 touched down and immediately braked hard to accommodate the shorter than normal runway of the Washington airport. It was a shame that federal law prohibited him from using his frequent flyer miles he accumulated during his official travel – God knows he owed Margie a vacation.

He was coming back from Charleston Air Force Base in South Carolina, where he had defended a master sergeant who had tested positive for recent cocaine use during a random urinalysis. Kuhn was not unhappy with his performance.

Although the sergeant had been convicted, Jack's advocacy had convinced the jury to impose a relatively light sentence – 30 days hard labor without confinement, a one stripe reduction in rank, and most importantly, NO punitive discharge. That meant his client would be able to retire and keep most of his military pension.

After his profoundly unhappy year plus in the Pentagon, Jack was thankful that the powers that be had put him back into a real legal job. As the head Air Force defense lawyer for the entire East Coast region of the United States, Jack had never been busier or, he knew, happier with his work. He got to try cases when he wanted to, he mentored – very effectively he thought – the many young circuit and area defense counsels under his supervision, and he got treated well whenever he was on the road, which was a lot. He'd been TDY, in fact, at least two weeks out of every month over the past year.

The last few months had been especially gratifying from a professional perspective, particularly when the promotion list to colonel was announced in mid-November. Although he'd allowed himself to hope and believe that he'd be promoted, there was simply no substitute for seeing one's name on the actual promotion list. And even though it might be almost two years before he pinned on his new rank, Kuhn knew he had literally beaten the odds when he was included among the 35% of JAG lieutenant colonels in his year group selected for advancement to 0-6.

He had also been buoyed by the fact that his longtime friend Larry Wilkins had been on the promotion list, the sole "below-the-zone" selectee on the list. Kuhn knew that Larry's early promotion unambiguously marked him as a prime contender for further promotions down the road.

He wished Margie had been happier about his own promotion, but he knew she was having a hard time right now, with him gone a lot, with Heather off to college at Southern Illinois University at Edwardsville (he'd kept his Illinois residency during all his time in service and thus Heather qualified for the significantly cheaper in-state tuition rate), and with Cindy not doing terribly well at Lake Braddock High. Plus, Margie clearly didn't like her current lot in life as a substitute teacher, a gig that occasionally took her into some of the very rough schools in and around DC.

Kuhn knew there were better times ahead, particularly when he pinned on colonel and they were reassigned out of DC in a couple of years. In the meantime, he thought, he hoped the bottle of Chardonnay in his carry-on bag and the crystalline unicorn figurine (Margie loved unicorns) he'd bought at the Charleston Base Exchange would suffice as a peace offering and expression of how much he cared for his wife and family.

Jack exited the plane and walked through the old Washington National terminal – he wondered if they'd ever get around to building a new one – to the Delta baggage conveyer, where he soon retrieved his one large suitcase and headed outside to get in line for a cab. On his way out, he saw a discarded USA Today on a plastic seat and snatched it up to read on the way home.

Friday rush hour was, no great shock, still heavy as the old green cab in which Jack rode made its way haltingly southward on the Shirley Highway, so he had plenty of time to read the paper. With all his attention and energy focused on his trial the past several days, he hadn't looked at a newspaper or watched the news since Monday.

Nothing much new on the front page, he thought. The lead story was conjecture about who President-elect Kemp intended to appoint for various cabinet-level positions in the new Administration. Kuhn had been on the road to McGuire AFB in New Jersey on Election Day last month, and despite having to be in court the next morning, had stayed up the better part of the night to watch the election returns. It had been a little closer than he had expected, but the former Buffalo Bills quarterback had beaten Massachusetts Governor Dukakis by about four percentage points when all was said and done. The greater surprise was that the Republicans had regained control of the Senate, albeit by a razor-thin 51-49 majority. The Democrats would still control the House of Representatives – *Democrats always control the House*, he thought – with a working majority of 30 seats over the GOP.

Kemp had promised during the campaign to halt the decade-long decrease in defense spending and to finally get inflation and unemployment under control. Kemp's campaign had reminded Jack and a lot of other folks of Ronald Reagan's twelve years earlier, minus the promise of a big tax cut, which no doubt would have been unrealistic given the currently burgeoning national deficit. Hopefully, Jack thought, the fates will give Kemp more time to make good on those promises than they had the late 40th President of the United States.

At any rate, Jack thought, it was probably time for a political change in America – a majority of the electorate had thought so, anyway.

Seeing nothing else on the front page that piqued his interest, Jack rustled through the previously used newspaper for the sports section. He was disappointed to discover that section missing. *Occupational hazard of scrounging,* he thought.

He was not devastated. Being a lifelong Chicago sports fan, he knew the sports section rarely contained good news. Another dreadful Cubs season was now mercifully over, the Bears had failed again to make the playoffs, and the Bulls were still struggling around the .500 mark. The team to beat in the NBA right now (and for the foreseeable future) was the Portland Trailblazers with their superstar Michael Jordan, whom they'd selected with the second pick in the 1984 draft. As a former basketball player himself, Kuhn loved watching Jordan play, and thought he might be the best basketball player who ever lived. Jack sometimes allowed himself to fantasize about what the Bulls might have been like if they'd only had a slightly higher draft pick and been able to get Jordan for themselves. No use thinking about something that never happened, he chided himself as he terminated his NBA what-iffing.

After a while, Jack noticed that the cab was now well down Old Keene Mill Road, approaching the right turn on Lee Chapel Road that would take him to his townhouse. They arrived a couple minutes later, and Jack paid the cabby the fifty-five buck fare plus a five dollar tip (thank goodness he could claim such expenses on his travel voucher!)

Funny, he thought, no lights on. Maybe Margie and Cindy decided to splurge and go out for dinner somewhere, maybe at that new Denny's down by the Burke Center strip mall, he guessed.

He fumbled in the darkness for his house key. Finding it, he unlocked the front door and entered, setting his suitcase and carry-on down in the entryway.

"Anybody home?" he yelled up the stairs. Getting no answer, he flipped on some lights, and hauled his bags to the bedroom upstairs. Throwing the suitcase on their double bed, he took the bottle of wine and carefully wrapped figurine out of his carry-bag, and then walked back downstairs to position them on the kitchen table in order to surprise Margie.

Flipping on the overhead light as he walked into the kitchen, he turned to place his gifts. That's when he first noticed the two-page handwritten note sitting on the kitchen counter.

He gingerly picked up the letter as if it were a hand grenade with the pin pulled out. It was from Margie, of course, and it said that she and Cindy were driving to her folks' place in Missouri. Margie intended to enroll Cindy in school there next semester, the note said. Then the letter got much more emotional – Margie wrote that she could no longer stand living like a pauper in this God-forsaken place, and was fed up being married to a husband who was never home, one who cared more about his work than he did his wife and children. The last straw, she wrote, was when it became clear to her that he was going to accept promotion to colonel and, by definition, stay in the Air Force for several more years. She closed by asking Jack not to contact her or the girls until after the holidays, at which time they could begin to discuss the details of the split.

Jack staggered into the small living room and fell back into his beat-up old Lazy Boy like he'd been hit upside the head with a baseball bat. He couldn't remember ever having shed a tear in all of his adult life – holding Margie's note in his hand, however, he started to sob uncontrollably. He didn't stop for fifteen minutes.

CHAPTER 20

Near Lawton, Oklahoma

8:45 p.m., November 13, 1994

Like each of the two dozen other men in the poorly lit old barn west of Lawton this particular Saturday night, 26-year-old Jonathan O'Neil was pissed off. A tall man in blue jeans and a tee shirt emblazoned with a swastika superimposed over an American flag stood in front of the group, most of whom were seated on metal folding chairs or crates.

The tall man was talking and occasionally shouting, and O'Neil thought he was making a lot of sense. The American dream *had* been hopelessly corrupted by the Jews, the blacks, the homos, the illegal aliens, and by the two socialist political parties in this country that continually conspired with that evil constituency to take away the rights and hard-earned dollars of real Americans.

The tall man was right, too, about the real enemy not being in Moscow or Peking, but in Washington, D.C., where the President and Congress plotted every day to come up with new taxes to finance the FBI, CIA, and ATF which kept them in power, and to underwrite lavish new entitlement programs for the lazy and least deserving.

Like everyone else in the room, O'Neil cheered wildly when the speaker produced a picture of President Kemp, pulled out a cigarette lighter, and then set the picture on fire, dropping it into a bucket at his feet. Kemp had turned out to be a wolf in sheep's clothing, Jonathan knew. The President had campaigned in 1992 promising to make the country strong again, a place where traditional American values would once again prevail, Jonathan remembered bitterly. Had he been registered, in fact, O'Neil probably would have voted for Kemp – *what a mistake that would have been!*

O'Neil's blood literally boiled when he remembered how less than two months in office, the Republican President had shown his true colors by ordering his FBI and ATF goons to storm the Branch Davidian compound in Waco and massacre David Koresh and so many others. O'Neil raged at the memory of the vicious federal attack that had ended the ten-day standoff and left the Davidian leader and nineteen of his followers dead. Jonathan had no doubt that the rumors that Koresh had initially been captured, then summarily executed by FBI hit men after two hours of interrogation, were true.

The speaker in the tee shirt was right about everything, O'Neil realized. The Founding Fathers would have never put up with the kind of oppression that existed in America today. They would have taken up arms. That's the whole reason, Jonathan knew, why the Second Amendment had been enacted in the first place, to make sure that patriotic citizens would have the guns and weapons necessary to overthrow a corrupt and immoral government.

O'Neil knew guns and weapons, of course, from his time in the Army – he'd been a gunner on a Bradley fighting vehicle and had seen a little action in Panama in 1989. But that was before he'd realized that the United States Army was but another cog in the evil federal machine that enslaved the country. He'd taken an early-out right after the war, and was damn glad he had.

Although the last couple years had been hard ones – he'd moved around a lot after deciding there was nothing for him to stick around for back home in Pennsylvania – he knew he was now much stronger for the experience. And his strength would be critical if the revolution that lie ahead was to succeed.

The tall man then said something that hadn't occurred to O'Neil. *Maybe the rebellion really is already underway*. Maybe the bombings of abortion clinics around the country, the shooting of the judge and the U.S. Attorney in Los Angeles, the battles at Ruby Ridge and Waco, and the car bomb at the Army recruiting station in Chicago were just the opening salvos. Maybe the people were already starting to rise up, however tentatively. The speaker was right about everything else, Jonathan knew – it made sense that he was right about this too.

Suddenly, O'Neil knew what he had to do, what he would do. Every revolution needed a defining early victory, a truly spectacular attack not only to slay as many of the enemy as possible, but also to unmistakably demonstrate to the population that the time for action had now come.

And Jonathan knew the perfect target, an enemy building one hundred miles or so north of where he sat. It housed many of the different agencies that viciously continued to prop up the decaying federal dictatorship. The FBI was there, he was pretty sure, and so were the IRS, ATF, GSA, military recruiters, and many more. It was ideal.

And he knew how to do it, too. He'd read how you could use fuel and fertilizer to make a bomb - it looked easy. And he'd make a big one, by God, a lot bigger than the puny car bomb in Chicago a couple of weeks ago that only killed three military recruiters or the other one in Atlanta that only broke windows.

There'll probably be some unavoidable collateral damage from a real big bomb, he thought, but that couldn't be avoided. There were always unintended innocent casualties in every war, and especially wars of liberation.

He'd need a little help, of course, but he had a couple of old Army buddies he thought he could trust. And although it might take a few months to get everything ready, he'd make damn sure his attack was worth the wait.

O'Neil allowed himself to fantasize about the statue that would no doubt be erected someday in his honor in Oklahoma City. He was going to be a Founding Father himself, a founding father of the New America.

CHAPTER 21

Tinker Air Force Base
Oklahoma City, Oklahoma
1000 hours, 19 April 1995

This was the part of trial Jack hated most, the "hanging around" period while the jury deliberated his client's guilt or innocence. There was now absolutely nothing he could do to influence events or outcomes – his only current duty was to wait while the jury did its job.

Jack, in fact, dreaded any period of time in which he found himself not fully occupied - that's when his idle mind invariably turned into his enemy and his pain took center stage. Although it had been two years now since Margie left him and took Cindy with her, Jack still badly missed his wife. No, he reminded himself, *make that my ex-wife.* When his mind wasn't focused on something else, it would concoct insipidly stupid schemes to get her back. Or remind him of his current demeaning lifestyle sharing a run-down two-bedroom apartment in Rosslyn with another JAG whose wife had left him, or his regular evening meal routine at McDonald's or Burger King. Or zap him with the painful memories of the divorce process, in which Margie's pit bull of a lawyer had tried (pretty damn successfully, Jack knew) to suck every last ounce of blood from him. Or conjure up some new horrible explanation as to why his youngest daughter Cindy seemed to treat him with such an emotionless lack of interest when he called her every week.

Jack Kuhn much preferred to be as busy as humanly possible, and on the road as much as he could get away with. He knew he personally defended far more "away" cases than any of the Air Force's other four CCDCs. While his zeal probably appeared to many to be the product of dedication, Jack knew it was really his means of escape. He even frequently volunteered to take cases outside his own circuit when he could fit them in his already crammed schedule.

This was one such case. Tinker Air Force Base was in the Central Circuit, not the Eastern Circuit that Jack headed. But someone had recommended Colonel (select) Kuhn's name to the sergeant being court-martialed, who had then requested that Jack be made available to serve as his defense counsel. Since Jack wouldn't pin on his eagles for another month, he was happy to take one more case before moving on to his next assignment.

It was really a pretty interesting case, Jack thought. His client was in court because he'd beat the crap out of another Air Force sergeant one night in a bar in Norman, Oklahoma, a few miles from the base. The victim, whose jaw was badly broken, happened to be gay. What made the case interesting was that the government had opted to prosecute it not as a simple or aggravated assault, but rather as a "hate crime" assault under the recently enacted Article 128A of the Uniform Code of Military Justice, thus converting the normal maximum punishment from six months in jail to ten years.

That there'd been a fight was indisputable, as was the fact that his client had thrown the haymaker that broke the gay sergeant's jaw in two places. Where the government's case broke down, Jack hoped, was on the issue of specific intent – to convict under Article 128, the prosecution had to prove beyond a reasonable doubt that his client committed the assault because of the victim's sexual orientation.

The prosecution offered up only two really damaging pieces of testimony in support of their theory. An airman first class testified that he heard the accused tell an offensive homosexual joke about a month prior to the incident, and the victim testified that the sergeant had called him a "fag" during the course of their scuffle.

On cross-examination, Jack had been able to get the victim to admit that he'd never met the accused before that night, and that the fight started shortly after he'd inadvertently spilled a drink on the accused. Jack was also able to elicit from the victim that both participants had been drinking heavily that evening.

During the defense portion of the case, Jack put the accused on the stand, not something he did in every case. He admitted telling the offensive joke, and also conceded he'd had at least a half dozen gin and tonics before the fight. He claimed to have only a fuzzy recollection of the fight itself, and didn't remember calling the victim a "fag." On cross examination, the prosecutor did what Jack hoped she would, and asked the accused if it was possible he might have called the victim a "fag" during the fight. To her surprise, and Jack's satisfaction, the accused said he might have used the term, but that it was not unusual for him and his circle of friends, none of whom were gay, to call each other "fags" when they wanted to "pull somebody's chain."

Jack was happy with the closing argument he'd given, pointing out absence of meaningful evidence regarding intent, the various reasonable alternatives to the prosecution's theory. Who among everybody in the courtroom, Jack rhetorically asked, hadn't told or at least laughed at a homosexual joke at some point in their lives. And for how many generations of humanity had young men engaged in lowbrow but meaningless trash talk.

There was absolutely no evidence, Jack further pointed out, that his client selected the victim on the basis of sexual orientation. Wasn't it just as reasonable to believe, Jack asked, that this was simply a case where one drunk took a swing at another who spilled a drink on his new leather jacket. Jack also pointed out that his client had been far too drunk to have been able to form the specific intent necessary to commit the crime with which he had been charged. He closed by accusing the prosecution of "overreaching" by trying to turn political incorrectness into a felony by inappropriately using Article 128 to jack up the maximum punishment.

In truth, Jack believed most of his argument (that wasn't always the case when one was a defense counsel) and was convinced that his client really had been too drunk to give a good goddamn about the gay sergeant's orientation. But he also knew that what he believed wasn't important – it was what the jury believed that mattered.

Based on the evidence presented during the two-day trial and what he thought had been a good closing argument, Kuhn was actually pretty confident that his client wouldn't be found guilty of the "hate crime" assault under 128A. He thought it probable, however, the jury might find him guilty of the lesser included offense of simple assault, which carried a maximum punishment of only six months. Under military law, at least five of the seven-person jury had to vote to convict in order for his client to be found guilty of either charge. If fewer than five voted to convict, the accused would be declared not guilty.

Based on the body language of the jurors during his argument, Jack hoped he'd convinced at least three of them that the government had failed to meet its burden of proof beyond a reasonable doubt. He kept his fingers crossed.

Shortly before 1100 hours, the bailiff let Jack know that court was about to reconvene. He hurried back to the courtroom down the hall, and quickly took his seat – his client was already there.

Jack and the sergeant rose when the judge reentered, and rose again two minutes later when the judge instructed the President of the jury to read the verdict.

"Sergeant Thompson, this court-martial finds you not guilty," came the hoped for words from the colonel who was the senior member of the panel. Jack smiled at his client, and was reaching to shake his hand when the building's windows suddenly rattled to the sound of an incredibly loud "boom."

The judge hastily adjourned the court, walked from his bench, and opened the blinds of the large window on the north side of the courtroom.

They all saw it instantly. In the direction of Oklahoma City twenty miles to the northwest, a huge plume of dark smoke rose menacingly into what was otherwise a cloudless blue sky.

CHAPTER 22

The Kremlin, Moscow, USSR
1130 p.m., April 30, 1996

As he alternately read and edited the text in front of him, it occurred to Mikhail Gorbachev that this particular evening felt a lot like some from his university days so many years ago, when he paid for occasional academic procrastination by working through the night to prepare for an examination the following day. He was mildly annoyed at himself for putting this task off as long as he had. He had been thinking for months, in fact, about the May Day address he'd be giving tomorrow evening to the citizens of the USSR.

There were some things he intended to say that he simply could not have told his speechwriters in advance, hence the need for his personal involvement this day and night to carefully craft the final version of the speech.

It had been an excellent year, and he had much to report to the citizenry. The current economic boom his country was now enjoying had been a long time coming, the result, he knew, of the difficult reforms he had initiated ten years ago. It had not been easy to convert traditional (but disastrously nonsensical) communist economic theory and practice into the consumer-oriented, incentive-based economic communism he had envisioned, but the proof of the correctness and viability of his vision was now there for everyone to see throughout his huge country. Consumer goods had never been more plentiful or affordable for the Soviet people, their standard of living never higher, and the long awaited (and badly belated, in Gorbachev's view) systematic exploitation of the abundant natural resources of Siberia was now fully underway, promising to keep the USSR's economic engine running at full speed for many years to come.

His country had come a very long way from the dark days of the mid 1980's, when the USSR demonstrated by very painful example the first rule of major change – sometimes things have to get worse before they get better. In fact, things had gotten much worse, and truth be known, his nation had come perilously close to ruination. Due, he knew, to some astute political decision-making on his part, as well as some good fortune, the Soviet Union had nevertheless emerged from those dark depths to where it found itself now – economically stronger than it had ever been in its history.

Likewise, Gorbachev thought, the international security situation could scarcely be better from his country's point of view. The unification of Germany some eighteen months earlier had been the final lynchpin, he thought with considerable satisfaction.

The negotiations had taken the better part of four years. It wasn't until after the death of Honecker in East Germany and the election of leftist Schroeder in West Germany that the conditions were finally right to conclude the reunification treaty, with both sides finally able agree to the one condition that the Soviets had insisted upon. That condition was withdrawal of all occupying forces (Soviet, American, British, and French) from Germany within 12 months of the agreement.

From Gorbachev's point of view, the reunification agreement was win-win-win-win. First, maintaining Soviet troops in East Germany had become a very expensive proposition – a significant drain on the USSR's defense budget had now been eliminated. Secondly, the Soviets – who obviously had long-standing economic ties with the eastern half of reunited Germany – now had a leg up when it came to doing business with a larger German trading partner whose currency had real substance.

Thirdly, removal of the last American military bases in West Germany, particularly Ramstein Air Base near Kaiserslautern and the U.S. Army base at Schweinfurt, removed a major military irritant to his country, and effectively pushed U.S. forces back to the other side of the English Channel.

And finally, with a unified Germany obligated to assume a lesser "associate" relationship (much like the French) with the North Atlantic Treaty Organization, NATO was now effectively neutered and posed no real military danger to the countries of Eastern Europe. Gorbachev thought it very possible, in fact, that NATO might well implode on its own and dissolve in the not-to-distant future. With America having greatly reduced its presence on the continent over the past decade, with the victories of both the Spanish and Italian socialists in recent parliamentary elections, and with the Turks' well known "flexibility" when it came to alliances (depending on which way they thought the wind was blowing), the only major European military power still really committed to NATO was Britain. And Gorbachev knew how much most of the countries on the continent despised assuming any subservient role to *that* particular island nation.

He also knew that President Kemp, no matter how much he disliked the trend of events in Europe in general and Germany in particular, had been powerless to object, particularly when the entire world watched the incredibly powerful TV images of joyous Germans (soldiers and civilians alike) from both former countries physically tearing down the wall that had divided their nation for so long.

Things were also good, Gorbachev thought with some considerable satisfaction, throughout Eastern Europe, where most of the communist countries that flanked the USSR's western border were also enjoying relatively good economic times.

The Polish labor movement had posed some problems a few years ago, but appointing Lech Walesa, the movement's leader, as Minister of Labor for the Polish government had been a stroke of genius, effectively co-opting him. The damning videotape taken by Polish investigators of Walesa taking a huge bribe less than a year later had made his political tenure a short one, and his labor movement had quietly collapsed into oblivion about the same time he was heading off to prison. Gorbachev had never bothered to confirm one way or the other whether the KGB played any role in Walesa's demise – it really didn't matter, anyway.

Likewise, Rumania was now stable after some rumblings of discontent in 1990. Gorbachev had no doubt that most Rumanians still despised Ceausescu and his idiot wife, but the strongman's exceptionally firm response to the dissidents and their incipient uprising (without any military help from the Soviets, by the way) had left an indelible impression on his people regarding the very high cost of reactionary activism.

Yugoslavia continued to be a source of some worry, but Milosevic still appeared to have things under control in his dangerously diverse country. The Muslim Bosnians, the Croats, and the native Albanians in Kosovo occasionally continued to agitate for independence, but thus far the Serb had been able to keep those divisive ethnic ambitions largely in check, due both to his deserved reputation for ruthlessness toward his enemies as well as some judicious grants of limited autonomy to the provinces of Bosnia and Croatia. The German reunification treaty had made Milosevic's job a good deal easier when it became unmistakably clear to potential revolutionaries in Yugoslavia that a now toothless NATO couldn't and wouldn't ever come to their rescue if they crossed the line with the Yugoslavian chief executive.

Gorbachev remembered immodestly how he, too, had skillfully and effectively played the "autonomy" card, in his case with the occasionally troublesome Baltic Republics within his own country. He had two years ago granted Estonia, Latvia, and Lithuania a bit more in the way of local self-determination. That small concession, when combined with the dramatic and visible improvement in the standard of living throughout the USSR, had successfully quieted most of the voices of discontent in those three small Soviet republics.

It was amazing, thought Gorbachev not for the first time, how many political problems simply disappear, or at least diminish to a non-threatening level, when economic times are good and people perceive that their lives are getting better.

Gorbachev looked up from the text he'd been working on, rubbed his eyes, and leaned back in his desk chair, fixing his gaze on the two pictures on the wall that captured both of his Nobel Peace Prizes. He'd shared the first with Mondale for their Nuclear Reduction Treaty in 1988, and received the second three years later for his deft resolution of the Iraq-Kuwait mess in 1991.

The latter accomplishment, and the subsequent business and military relationship that he had built with the Saudis as a result, was a source of extreme satisfaction to Gorbachev. King Fahd, if not exactly an ally in the traditional sense, was nevertheless now at least a very valuable customer. The rich contract for the sale of nearly 120 Soviet MIG-29s over the next five years, along with all necessary training and aircraft support services, to the Royal Saudi Air Force was but the latest example. And with the USSR continuing to serve as the Kingdom's ad hoc guarantor against any future Iraqi mischief aimed in the Saudi's direction, Gorbachev was supremely confident the broadened Soviet-Saudi relationship would continue to grow further.

With Syria, Iraq, and Saudi Arabia, and to a lesser extent Egypt and Kuwait, now all decidedly pro-USSR in their outlook, the Middle East was a region of grand opportunity for his nation. Indeed, with Yasir Arafat now dead more than three years from that Libyan plane crash, and with the dovish general Ehud Barak the likely next prime minister of Israel, Gorbachev thought there might even be a window of opportunity in the near future to settle the Palestine question once and for all. That'd be worth ten Nobel Peace prizes, he laughed to himself.

The only really dangerous Soviet enemy left in the Middle East, knew Gorbachev, was Iran. With its huge population base of 65 million people, significant oil riches, and aggressively fundamentalist pan-Islamic theology, Iran was the proverbial festering sore on the underbelly of the USSR. Without question, the Iranians were responsible for the continuing difficulties that continued to beset the pro-Soviet government in neighboring Afghanistan, both by helping to fund and arm the terrorist bandits and by providing them sanctuary on the Iranian side of the mountainous border between the two countries. Even more troubling were the obvious Iranian designs and ambitions with regard to the several largely Muslim southern republics of the USSR. The populations of Turkmenistan and Azerbaijan were, Gorbachev feared, especially susceptible to Iranian influence. Indeed, there was strong suspicion on the part of KGB analysts that Iran had played a supporting role in the recent deadly bombing of a government building in Grozny by Chechnyan terrorists. Iran would, he knew, have to be dealt with one of these days.

Iran was, of course, the reason Gorbachev had worked so hard to extract Saddam and his army from their incredibly foolish Kuwait adventure. Having a militarily strong and potentially threatening Iraq sitting adjacent to Iran's western frontier was of inestimable value, Gorbachev knew – it took a good deal of pressure off the Soviet's southern republics bordering Iran by forcing the Islamic Republic to spend its time and resources preparing to defend themselves against the vitriolic Saddam.

And then there was America. The United States no longer represented the imminent threat to his country that it once did, thought the general-secretary with unabashed pride. Gorbachev's initially controversial policies of *glasnost* and *perestroika* had turned out to be brilliantly successful in dramatically diminishing the perception of the danger the USSR posed to America and indeed much of the world. That, and his irresistible invitation to America to focus and aggressively pursue its foreign policy objectives within its own hemisphere during the 1980s, had gone a long way toward creating the kind of world Gorbachev had envisioned when he came into office a decade ago. Gorbachev also knew that the U.S. was currently excessively preoccupied trying to put a stop to the spate of home-grown terror attacks within its own borders. The worst, of course, had been the huge truck bomb that demolished the federal building in Oklahoma, killing almost 200 men, women, and children.

In a strange way, he sympathized with President Kemp. Had he been elected ten years earlier, his effort to rebuild the American military might have made a difference. Now, however, American military power was largely superfluous, at least in those parts of the world that were important to the Soviet Union. There was really nothing for Kemp or America to do with a bigger or better army now. Invade a finally reunified Germany to bring it back fully into the NATO fold? Seize the oil fields of Saudi Arabia or Iraq or Kuwait? "Liberate" an increasingly prosperous Eastern Europe?

No, thought Gorbachev, the massive geo-political gains he'd skillfully orchestrated over the last decade, most without overt use of the indisputably powerful Soviet military machine, were simply not now realistically susceptible to being militarily undone by America. Gorbachev suspected Kemp would be held accountable next year by the American electorate for his anachronistic and expensively misdirected focus on trying to rebuild American military power.

In point of fact, Gorbachev had never wanted to "destroy" the United States. What he had always wanted, what he had worked so hard to cultivate, was an America that was strong enough to defend itself, but not so strong as to pose a direct military threat to his nation's vital interests. An America whose economy was healthy enough to be a viable trading partner with the USSR and a lucrative market for its products, but not so strong economically so as to be able to leverage its wealth to influence events in ways not advantageous to his nation.

All things considered, ruminated Gorbachev, things simply could not be going better for the Soviet Union. At the bottom line, even though his nation still shared the title "superpower" with America, momentum was now clearly in the Soviet's favor, a judgment shared by much of the rest of the world based on their rush to accommodate that new reality.

He would enjoy giving his upbeat address to his comrade citizens tomorrow, and was especially looking forward to its dramatic conclusion – the part his speechwriters didn't know and therefore hadn't written – in which he would announce his resignation and the appointment of Vladimir Putin as his successor. What could possibly be better than going out "on top," thought Gorbachev. And that was exactly what he'd do tomorrow night.

CHAPTER 23

Offutt Air Force Base
Omaha, Nebraska
0700 hours, 15 December 1996

The funny thing about cold wars, thought Colonel Kuhn, was that nobody had ever figured out how they're supposed to end. As he drove into work through the main gate at Offutt AFB, his eyes automatically turned to the spotlighted Minuteman III missile (static display, of course) that symbolically stood watch in front of the Strategic Air Command headquarters building a quarter mile ahead.

Even if the Soviet Union's much-ballyhooed facelift and current kinder, gentler image had now pushed the Cold War to the back recesses of public consciousness, Jack knew that the USSR still had a lethal nuclear arsenal pointed in this direction. And as long as that was so, SAC would continue to keep America's own nuclear missiles and bombers at the ready. While no one he knew seriously thought that nuclear war between the United States and the USSR was even a remote possibility these days, it was a historical truism that the only proven way to prevent one nuclear power from using that horrific power was the ability and willingness to unleash a similar horror upon the aggressor. With all its implicit irony, that fundamental truth was the core belief of SAC, whose long-time motto was "Peace is our Profession." And SAC, Kuhn knew, had made good on that motto by preserving the peace – at least nuclear peace – for all of its almost fifty-year history.

No, Jack didn't think there really *was* an endgame to the Cold War. Even if relations between the superpowers continued to thaw and all mutual malice eventually evaporated, and even if the two long-time adversaries continued to reduce their nuclear arsenals, he imagined that fifty years from now the officer and enlisted personnel of SAC would still be standing watch, professionally and dispassionately, against the Soviet Union, whose military would in turn be standing a similar watch against America. Jack thought the famous line from "The Godfather" was apropos – *it's not personal, it's just business.*

Jack drove past the Minuteman display and the headquarters building, turning left to head to the northern part of the base where he spent his workdays. Now a full colonel, the JAG was once again a Staff Judge Advocate in charge of a SAC legal operation, this time the 55th Strategic Wing Legal Office. It was, of course, a much larger office than he had run at Wurtsmith over a decade ago – he now supervised almost thirty military lawyers and paralegals and was responsible for providing a full range of legal services to the huge Nebraska base.

He'd been delighted to be reassigned to this place and these duties last year when the Air Force mercifully concluded at long last that he had paid enough DC dues, at least for now. Despite his profound unhappiness with DC in general and with his initial Pentagon gig working for the Inspector General, the last three years as Chief Circuit Defense Counsel had been both professionally challenging and highly rewarding. From a personal standpoint, of course, DC had been the low point of his life as he was forced to abruptly adjust to single life after Margie had devastated him by leaving. *Has it really been almost three years since she left?* He wondered.

But he had learned to cope (and cook some, believe it or not!), and his demanding CCDC duties had fortunately left him little time to wallow in self-pity. Whoever coined the phrase "shit happens" knew what they were talking about, as far as Jack was concerned. The trick, Jack knew, was being able to move on in spite of whatever fecal mess life threw in your way.

Reassignment to Nebraska had also permitted him the realistic opportunity to see his grown daughters on a somewhat regular basis.

Heather was now 23, and had graduated from SIUE last year with a degree in nursing. She now lived in a small apartment she shared with another young nurse close to the Belleville, Illinois, hospital where they both worked. Cindy was 21 and still lived with her mother and new stepfather (Margie had married another lawyer, albeit a civilian one, late last year – *she's a real glutton for punishment* he thought) about 40 miles from Heather, across the river in O'Fallon, Missouri.

Unlike her older sister, Cindy was still struggling to "find herself." She'd barely graduated from high school, spent a year (more or less, based on the reports Jack had gotten from her sister) attending a local junior college to be close to her boyfriend at the time, and since gone through a series of largely dead-end jobs. She was currently working as a night manager for a yogurt place in O'Fallon.

Unfortunately, Cindy and that scumbag significant other (now thankfully long departed) had also made Jack and Margie unwilling grandparents six months ago, though neither he nor his ex-wife were ever likely to see or know their first grandchild. Cindy's out of wedlock baby had been immediately put up for adoption through a placement agency in St. Louis – Jack didn't have a clue where and with whom the child had landed. He sometimes imagined that in a different reality, one in which he and Margie were still together, they'd have adopted Cindy's baby themselves and raised it as their own.

Margie's remarriage had been a hurtful surprise to Jack, though honestly not as pervasively painful as their protracted divorce had been. It had, at least, allowed him to mentally close the book on the far-fetched prospect of reconciliation he had stupidly allowed himself to hope and wish for. And it had also put a good deal more money in his pocket when his monthly alimony obligations were terminated upon her remarriage. He'd gotten another welcome "raise" when he'd made Heather's final college tuition payment last year.

That happy improvement in his financial circumstance had allowed him to do something a few months ago he'd never before done – buy a brand new car. He and the Offutt Credit Union were co-owners of a semi-sporty 1996 Toyota Camry which had cost him a cool $38,000. Although the little red car wouldn't have been big enough when he'd been married, it was fine for a single guy. And it got 36 miles per gallon on the open road.

That was important when he made his monthly sojourn to the St. Louis area to see his daughters. With the price of unleaded gas vacillating between two and half and three dollars a gallon, a few extra miles a gallon made a big difference over the 900-mile round trip.

He had his "visitation" routine down to a precise science. Every month or so, he'd depart Offutt right after work on Friday, drive down I-29 to Kansas City to catch I-70 toward St Louis, then get on I-64 to cross the Mississippi River toward Scott AFB, where he'd pull in (usually before midnight) to the Billeting Office and get a key for one of the relatively inexpensive DV quarters the base maintained for colonels and above.

On Saturdays, he'd meet up with his daughters around noon, usually at Heather's place in nearby Belleville, spend the afternoon at the mall or a matinee, and grab an early dinner (their current favorite was Joe's Crab Shack just off the interstate by the mall) in time for the girls to pursue whatever social plans they'd made for that particular Saturday night. Those plans invariably did not include Jack, who fully understood the compelling social needs of good-looking twenty-something young ladies. On those rare occasions when one or the other did not have plans, they'd typically spend the evening on one of the half dozen or so casino "riverboats" that were "anchored" – they really were built on concrete pillars – near the MLK bridge over the Mississippi, usually pissing away a hundred dollars or so before calling it a night.

The following morning, they'd almost always meet at the Scott Officers Club to chow down on the excellent and ample Sunday brunch the club offered, after which Jack would kiss them goodbye and hit the road back to Omaha, to arrive back before 8 p.m., tired but contented in the renewed knowledge he was still a practicing father, and not a half bad one at that.

He wished, though, that he could do more to help Cindy find her way – it was obvious to him that she was a young lady who right now was adrift in the sea of life. She'd experienced more than her share of bad karma, Jack thought with paternal sympathy – she'd taken the divorce harder than her older sister, and getting pregnant shortly thereafter had obviously also been emotionally difficult for her.

And like all fathers in this day and age, he supposed, he wondered and worried whether she might be sometimes seeking temporary refuge in illegal drugs like marijuana that were so common an escape for youngsters these days. She had always denied any such involvement, of course, but Jack wished he had a higher degree of confidence in the sincerity of those denials.

He tried not to be too judgmental during their father-daughter talks, both on the phone and when they visited, gently encouraging her to go back to school in order to expand her opportunities beyond the $5.30 an hour minimum wage jobs that were her current lot in life.

She usually seemed to respond positively during those conversations, though she invariably pointed out to him that the America in which she was now trying to find her place didn't present the same opportunities as when he was starting his own adult journey almost three decades ago. She was right about that, of course, but he worried that the implicit negativity of that truism had grown into her personal universal excuse.

Cindy had never, Jack knew, responded particularly well to in-your-face direction and guidance – that was something her mother had never seemed to understand, Jack remembered, thinking back to their frequent acrimonious verbal spats during Cindy's teenage years. Knowing his youngest daughter's personality as he did, Jack had worked hard since the split to keep their dialogue going in as positive and non-threatening a way as he could muster. He had also continued to occasionally supplement her finances as best he could, but the $98,000 a year he made as an Air Force colonel only went so far these days.

Between the incessantly insistent demands of his military duties and the time-consuming paternal obligations he cherished so much, Jack hadn't had much time for much of a social life the past couple of years. He'd been on some dates, of course, a few of the "set-up" variety, but had found no one that lit his candle like Margie had done. And while he appreciated (and needed!) the occasional hormonal release that his social encounters sometimes provided, he was still leery about getting too close to any woman right now. In fact, he doubted very much that he'd ever get married again, a personal prediction that caused him no great sorrow.

His life was not perfect, he knew, nor were the lives of those he loved and had loved. And although Margie was long gone, he knew he was still happily – some would say fanatically – married to his work and to being a JAG. As he pulled into the reserved parking space next to his office, he realized that there were lots worse things than loving what you did for a living.

Sadly, the worst possible thing was waiting for Kuhn as he walked in his office this day. The wing commander and the base chaplain were there to somberly convey the tragic news that his youngest daughter had died, apparently of a drug overdose, last night.

CHAPTER 24

The White House, Washington, D.C.
9:00 a.m., May 15, 1998

He had waited so long to get here, thought President Albert Gore of Tennessee. Had he known the amount of petty BS he'd end up having to deal with, however, he might have decided to remain in political retirement rather than run in 1996.

No, he corrected himself, had he'd stayed on the sidelines, it was likely that the hormonally challenged SOB he was about to talk to would now be President of the United States. Gore couldn't even imagine what that would be like.

It had been as close a primary campaign as the country had seen in over a half a century, President Gore remembered. He'd only had about 45% of the delegates in his corner going into the convention in Chicago; Arkansas' oft-time governor Bill Clinton, whom Gore had to grudgingly admit had conducted an awfully effective campaign for one who had never held elective office outside of his home state, had the support of about a third of the voting delegates. The surprise of the campaign season had been the political novice Ralph Nader, whose innovative "consumer populism" had caught on with a sizeable minority of the electorate who eagerly bought into his message that corporate America was to blame for the country's intransigent economic woes. To the shock and dismay of Democratic Party regulars, Nader had come to the convention with nearly 15% of the delegates committed to him.

Clinton had courted Nader hard just before the convention, Gore remembered. Fortunately, no matter how hard they tried, Clinton's number-crunchers ultimately were forced to conclude that even with

Nader's delegates, Arkansas Bill would still fall short of the target needed to win the nomination. That left the Clinton people no viable option other than to come hat in hand to Gore and offer Clinton's delegates in exchange for the vice-presidential nomination.

Given Gore's personal and visceral dislike of Nader, and the fact that the erstwhile consumer advocate had loudly declared that he wouldn't consider releasing his delegates until after the first ballot, Gore had likewise seen little option at the time other than to accept Clinton's offer. It was absolutely crucial that the Party be as unified as possible going into the general election, and he couldn't risk the uncertainty and potential chaos that might ensue if the convention was unable to select a nominee on the first ballot.

He'd been aware, of course, of the Arkansas governor's reputation for applying an extremely liberal interpretation to his marriage vows, but had been confident that Clinton's burning ambition to be president someday would convince him of the need to keep his well-known libido henceforth in check. If he had only known then, Gore thought bitterly, what he knew now.

Compared to getting his party's nomination, the general election had been a cakewalk. Gore and Clinton, who had in fairness been a great campaigner for the Democratic ticket, had effectively painted President Kemp and Vice President Lugar as slaves to old ideas that had no relevance to a country preparing to enter a new Millennium. Kemp never came within ten percentage points in the polls leading up to Election Day, and Gore's eventual 56-44% popular vote victory was almost anti-climactic.

The small speaker box on Gore's desk chirped. "Mr. President, the Vice President is here for his appointment," said the disembodied female voice.

"Send him in," said the President coldly in the direction of the box.

The door to the Oval Office opened two seconds later, and Vice President William Jefferson Clinton strode in. "Good morning, Al," said Clinton.

"Sit down, Bill," replied Gore, trying hard not to verbalize the anger and frustration he felt.

Gore did not leave his desk. "I'm not going to beat around the bush, Bill," said Gore. Given the subject matter of this conversation, he immediately regretted the unintended innuendo, but continued, "I just got a copy of the FBI report. It says the semen stain on that young intern's dress matched your DNA. You obviously lied to the investigators when you denied having sex with her."

"Al, I did not have sex with that woman. I swear I didn't fuck her. She came on to me, and I let her give me head a couple of times. That's all there was to it."

"Are you out of your goddamn mind?" asked Gore incredulously.

"Listen, Al, I know I shouldn't have done it. But I honestly don't think it's that big a deal."

Gore still didn't really know his VP. Although it was frequently hard to pin down exactly where Clinton stood on issues, he was both book and street smart and had some good ideas. He also had an exceptional instinctive sense of which issues would resonate with the electorate. In fact, Gore thought, Clinton was probably as effective a campaigner as he had ever met, possessed of extraordinary personal charisma and able to connect on a very personal level with the voters. If only the bastard would have confined his "connecting" to the political arena, Gore wished.

"I want your resignation," Gore said icily.

"You've got to be kidding?" Clinton stammered in reply.

"I'm not. You've embarrassed me, you've embarrassed your family, you've embarrassed yourself, and you've recklessly threatened the ability of this administration to do the real work we need to be doing," responded Gore.

"And if I don't resign?" asked Clinton, trying to appear resolute.

"You'll be impeached and convicted," answered the President, with far more resolve. "After I withdraw my support, you'll be lucky if you get five votes in the Senate."

"Jesus Christ, Al, isn't there some other option?" asked Clinton, any pretense of resolution having instantly evaporated.

Gore ignored the stupid question. "Take this," commanded the President, sliding a piece of paper across his big desk in the direction of where Clinton sat.

It was a letter of resignation. "You'll say you're resigning for the good of the country, because as much as you'd like to defend yourself, you simply don't want to distract the Administration from the critical issues that need to be worked on behalf of the American people. I'll reluctantly accept your resignation, thank you for your long public service, and describe your decision to put the good of the country ahead of your own personal interests as 'courageous.' I'll try to keep this damn FBI report out of the public eye, but only so long as it doesn't leak from some lower level (*fat chance,* Gore thought sarcastically as he spoke). Beyond that, you're on your own."

"Can we talk about a presidential pardon?" asked a suddenly desperate soon-to-be ex-Vice President.

"Not a chance," Gore responded instantly. "I want your signed resignation by noon."

"Then I guess you'll have it, Mr. President," said Clinton softly, rising from his chair to leave.

As he reached the door, Clinton turned back toward Gore. "I'm sorry, Al."

"So am I, Bill," replied the President, turning in his chair to look out the window behind his desk.

CHAPTER 25

Bolling Air Force Base
Washington, D.C.
1000 hours, 24 July 1998

The call he'd received four months ago was the proverbial "bolt out of the blue." It wasn't every day that a mere colonel, particularly a JAG sitting in an office in Nebraska, got a telephone call directly from the Chief of Staff of the United States Air Force.

In this case, however, the CSAF had been Mick Casey, now a four-star general and newly appointed as the USAF's senior military officer. Casey had been his boss twice during Kuhn's career, and they'd gone to war together - and damn near gotten killed together - a decade earlier in Central America.

It had been over two years since he'd heard from Casey. The general had sent an extraordinarily lengthy and profoundly sensitive handwritten note of sympathy to Jack right after Cindy died. As he always did, Kuhn cringed and almost physically shuddered whenever anything reminded him of that horrific memory. Mercifully, such triggers now didn't occur quite as often as they used to.

"Jack, I need your help," Casey had told him without preamble.

"What can I do for you sir?" Kuhn had replied automatically.

"For starters, I want you to get on a C-21 I'm sending this afternoon and come to DC. I'd like to see you here in the Pentagon tomorrow morning. I've already cleared it with Charlie Robertson." Jack knew Casey was referring to the four star who currently commanded SAC, though Jack of course would never have deigned to use CINCSAC's first name himself.

"Anything I need to bring?" asked Jack, his head swimming at the thought that CSAF was sending a military Learjet to ferry him to the nation's capital.

"Just bring your legal mind, and an extra pair of underwear – I'll have a plane bring you back to Offutt tomorrow evening."

"Yes, sir," replied Kuhn, "can I ask the subject of the meeting?"

"Let's wait until we meet face to face to get into details," responded the Chief of Staff. "Come to think of it, though, you might want to get a copy of the Upshaw Report to read on the airplane."

"Will do, sir," replied Kuhn.

"See you tomorrow at 0900, Jack," General Casey had concluded.

Jack knew what the Upshaw Report, which had just been publicly released a few days earlier, was all about. After the terrorist bombing at Howard Air Force Base in Panama late last year, the Secretary of Defense – at the insistence of some members of the Senate Armed Services Committee - had appointed retired Marine general Andrew Upshaw to conduct an immediate inquiry into the facts and circumstances of the attack. Twenty-one Air Force enlisted personnel had been killed, most while they slept in their barracks, when a very large truck bomb was detonated on a street just outside the Howard AFB fence line.

Kuhn, in fact, had stumbled across CSPAN while channel surfing one evening last week and seen the tail end of the Congressional hearing at which Upshaw briefed his findings and recommendations to the Senate Armed Services Committee. The gist of those findings were essentially that the Howard commander, Brigadier General Stephen Emerson, had been criminally derelict by not anticipating such an attack and by failing to take "appropriate" action to prevent it or at least mitigate the damage and death.

Jack also remembered thinking at the time that it was a little unseemly how, immediately after the hearing had concluded, a smiling Upshaw had glad-handed and chatted up several of the Senators on the

SASC, almost as if he were a politician rather than the retired military officer he was.

Kuhn had been able to find and download the Report's eighty-page narrative from the DoD website. He'd spent almost all of the three-hour military flight from Offutt to Andrews Air Force Base reading the report.

He was struck by how little hard evidence the narrative seemed to cite in support of Upshaw's incredibly broad findings of culpability. There were, by the report's own admission, no specific warnings by the CIA or any other component of the American intelligence community that such an attack was likely. And despite the lack of any such specific indicators, the report acknowledged General Emerson had, in fact, unsuccessfully requested the local Panamanian authorities to close the road adjacent to the base several months before the attack took place. The report also noted that Emerson had taken a number of specific actions during his tenure to tighten security within the installation, specifically aimed at preventing potential terrorists from getting onto the base. Finally, Upshaw had conceded that the considerable fiscal pressures of a shrinking DoD budget had resulted in higher headquarters disapproval of some security measures that Emerson had proposed, including the building of new barracks further away from the Howard perimeter.

Despite all the evidence that Emerson had done more than any of his predecessors to protect his installation and the people he commanded, however, Upshaw's bottom line was harshly damning. Specifically, he recommended that the Secretary of the Air Force initiate disciplinary proceedings under the Uniform Code of Military Justice against Emerson and take administrative action against some above him in the chain of command.

One of Upshaw's several other recommendations catalogued at the end of the narrative caught Jack's attention. That particular recommendation, which suggested that DoD undertake a comprehensive program to procure new high-tech systems to facilitate force protection at all its installations, struck Jack as going well beyond Upshaw's investigative mandate.

The plane landed at Andrews Air Force Base just as the sun was setting. A young first lieutenant, one of the cadre of eager protocol officers at Andrews, saluted Jack as he got off the airplane, put his suitcase in the trunk of a staff car, gave him an envelope containing his room key, and sent him off with another salute. It was late enough so that the evening rush hour had already played itself out, and the twelve-mile trip westbound on the Beltway and then up I-295 to Bolling Air Force Base had taken less than twenty minutes. He'd been dropped off at the Columbia House at Bolling, normally used by traveling general officers and not colonels, Jack knew. General Casey had obviously directed that Colonel Kuhn be afforded first class treatment for this visit.

Per the note in his room, Jack was picked up the following morning by another staff car and driven to the Pentagon for his meeting with General Casey in his fourth floor E-ring office. He'd been ushered in at precisely 0900.

"Thanks for coming, Jack," Casey had said warmly as he stepped from behind his desk to greet him. Casey had motioned him to sit down at a small round table in the corner of the office, where Casey had joined him.

"Have you had a chance to look at General Upshaw's report?" asked CSAF.

"Yes sir. I was able to get through the narrative portion on the airplane."

"What's your take?" queried Casey.

"Frankly, sir, my first impression is that it's a real hatchet job. I didn't see much in the way of concrete evidence to support General Upshaw's recommendation that Emerson be drawn and quartered. It looks to me like Upshaw's got a real ax to grind."

Casey smiled. "Shack," CSAF responded, using the pilot-speak term meaning bull's-eye.

General Casey continued. "The problem is, Jack, that Upshaw's report now represents political truth, which in this town, as I'm sure you know, is more important than real truth. The Secretary of the Air Force has already ordered a follow-on investigation to look specifically at the issue of whether Steve Emerson should be court-martialed."

"How can I help?" asked Jack.

"You can serve as General Emerson's defense counsel," replied Casey. "I've recommended you to him."

"Of course, sir," said Jack, caught off-guard but trying to conceal that fact. "I assume that CINCSAC will make me available?" Jack asked, knowing full well that the Air Force chief would have already worked that particular detail.

"Charlie Robertson's already OK'd giving you up for a few months," had been CSAF's reply, as expected.

"There's a few other things you need to know," Casey had continued. "The first issue will be whether or not it's appropriate to court-martial or Article 15 General Emerson. Assuming the evidence does not ultimately support such disciplinary action, however, there's another issue. It hasn't been announced yet, but Steve Emerson has been selected for a second star. It's important to the Air Force that he get that star."

Jack listened as CSAF continued his analysis. "I've known Steve for a long time – he's a terrific commander who gets the mission done and takes great care of his people. I've looked at all the evidence about the bombing I can lay my hands on, and I can't see anything to suggest that he didn't do everything we expect a good commander to do."

"The problem," Casey went on, "is that real truth may not be enough to carry the day on this one. Whenever Congress is complicit when something bad happens, particularly when things aren't going particularly well for the country in general, you can be dead certain that they'll find a scapegoat to divert attention and take them off the hook."

"How is Congress complicit in this?" asked Kuhn.

"In at least two ways," explained the chief. "First of all, it's been Congress who has overseen gutting the intel community, particularly human intelligence, HUMINT, efforts – I'm convinced that's a big reason why the spooks couldn't give us any advance heads up that this kind of attack was likely. Secondly, for the last several years we've been trying to get increased funding for force protection, but Congress has shot down almost every proposal we've floated, at least the ones with major dollar signs attached to them."

"So, in other words, General Upshaw gave the folks on the Hill exactly what they wanted?" said Jack.

"Shack again. There's one other thing you probably need to know, but I don't want it to leave this room," commanded Casey. "Unless I become convinced that Steve Emerson really did something wrong or didn't do something that he should have, I'm going to fall on my sword if he doesn't get the second star he's already been selected for."

"You'd resign over this, sir?" asked Kuhn.

"You bet your sweet ass I would," emphatically responded the Chief. "At the end of the day, if I'm convinced that an Air Force commander did everything right and everything that we could have reasonably expected him to do, I'll be damned if I'll let that commander be crucified alone by the soulless political bastards in this Building and on the Hill."

Kuhn suddenly remembered why he and everybody else he knew who had ever worked for him would willingly follow General Mick Casey into hell and back.

"I'll do my best, sir," said Kuhn.

"I know you will, Jack. That's all I can ask. If there's anything you need while you're working this project, let my exec know."

After the meeting with CSAF, Kuhn had walked down the hall to meet his new client. After completing his tour as Howard commander, Brigadier General Emerson had been reassigned in February to the Pentagon to run a division for the Air Force director of personnel.

Jack flew back to Offutt later that day, and had spent the rest of the week cleaning up some projects at the office and briefing up his deputy, who would serve as acting SJA during Kuhn's absence. He'd returned to Washington the following Monday, this time via a United Airlines flight, carrying a much fuller suitcase.

He'd been assigned a room in the Mathies visiting officers quarters at Bolling, not nearly as nice as the Columbia House, of course, but still adequate. That room had now been his home for over a hundred days. The Judge Advocate General had allowed him to use a small office with a computer in the Carpenter Building on Bolling, which housed several divisions of the Air Force Legal Services Agency.

Kuhn and Emerson had since spent, Jack estimated, close to three hundred hours together in that office and the VOQ room working on the case. Kuhn had quickly concluded that General Casey was absolutely right about Steve Emerson – he was a terrific guy and, from everything Jack could see, a superbly dedicated Air Force officer. And the deeper Kuhn got into the case, the more he was convinced that his initial instinct about the Upshaw Report was correct – it was a classic case of intellectually flawed Monday morning quarterbacking, with precious little factual basis to support its apparently pre-ordained conclusions.

Most of the first eight weeks had been spent assembling mounds of documentary evidence, preparing excruciatingly detailed affidavits addressing the dozens of factual inaccuracies and omissions Kuhn had discovered in the Upshaw Report, and preparing Emerson for his testimony in late March to Lieutenant General Salter, who had been appointed by the Secretary of the Air Force to conduct the inquiry to determine whether Emerson should be court-martialed or otherwise disciplined.

Brigadier General Emerson's session testifying to General Salter in a small conference room at the Pentagon could not have gone better. He'd come across as the sincere and superb commander he was, patiently detailing his many actions to ensure force protection at Howard Air Force Base and cogently explaining the rationale behind all actions he took or did not take. Kuhn had been at Emerson's side throughout the five-hour marathon, but had had to do very little other than marvel at how well Emerson had been prepared.

Jack remembered thinking how different this case was from most he'd handled when he'd been a Chief Circuit Defense Counsel. In that job, he'd represented drug users, thieves, sexual offenders, and various other uniformed miscreants. This client, on the other hand, was indisputably smart, demonstrably ethical and dedicated, and possessed of absolute integrity. Further, this was the rarest of cases, one in which the full and complete no-BS truth was the defense's strongest weapon.

Their hard work had been rewarded when Salter issued his report in late April. Contrary to Upshaw's inflammatory sound-bite condemnation, Salter's lengthy report catalogued events and circumstances in scrupulously accurate detail, concluding among other things that there had been no specific warnings or indicators that Howard was to be the target of a terrorist attack.

Salter also found that the type of weapon used – a stand-off high explosive of significantly greater magnitude than that used by the American Nazi fanatic a few years earlier to destroy the federal building in Oklahoma City and kill almost two hundred people – could not have reasonably been anticipated or protected against. Salter's report also found that Emerson's prudent actions during his tenure to bolster force protection at Howard prevented the terrorists from actually getting their weapon onto the base, which no doubt had been their first choice, thus saving countless additional American lives who would have perished under such a scenario.

At the bottom line, the Air Force investigator found that Emerson had done the very best he could with the information and resources available to him, and unequivocally concluded that there was absolutely no factual basis to support disciplinary action.

Although the Salter report effectively eliminated any risk of court-martial for Emerson, it by no means assured that he'd be allowed to pin on the two-star rank he had already been chosen for.

In point of fact, Salter's conclusions had received a decidedly lukewarm reaction on the Hill. One SASC member, a Republican blowhard from Idaho whose IQ, Jack suspected, barely reached triple digits on a good day, had blasted the Air Force investigation as a cover-up and loudly opined that the earlier Upshaw report was worthier of belief. Likewise, Upshaw himself had been interviewed on CNN – he staunchly reiterated his original findings of culpability, and characterized Salter's subsequent report as "disappointing."

As a result, Jack had come to realize over the past week that Casey had been right, that "real" truth alone probably wouldn't carry the day for his client, at least when it came to the promotion he had earned and deserved. The JAG knew he had to find some persuasive "political truth" in order to convince the SASC that Emerson should be confirmed for promotion to major general.

He had struggled for days thinking through every detail of the case trying to come up with the proverbial silver bullet. He had almost abandoned hope when he remembered how one of Upshaw's recommendations – that Congress authorize the expenditure of substantial additional federal dollars to acquire high-tech force protection systems – had struck him as odd and somewhat out of place. Kuhn had a thought.

Excited, he'd immediately walked from the VOQ to his little office in the Carpenter Building just before midnight and turned on the computer. Double clicking on Internet Explorer, he went to the Gaggle search engine and typed in "Andrew Upshaw." With over 500 hits, it had taken several hours to find what his attorney instincts told him might be there. But he had found it – *that greedy son of a bitch*, Kuhn swore to himself, though not unhappily.

He spent another two hours, almost until sunrise, researching the hundreds of hits he received when he entered "Riveson Corporation." This search was a longer shot, he knew, but he hoped he might get lucky, real lucky. And he did.

Although Kuhn had told Steve Emerson he'd be talking to the SASC chief counsel, he intentionally had *not* told him the card he intended he play – there were sometimes things that lawyers had to do without the express consent of their clients.

Wearing a civilian suit instead of his uniform, he took a cab from Bolling to the Hart Building just northeast of the Capitol, and walked up to the second floor office of Stewart Walker, chief counsel to the Senate Armed Services Committee. He was eventually ushered into Mr. Walker's office a half hour later.

"Thanks for seeing me, Mr. Walker," Kuhn had started. He was initially amazed at Walker's youth – he couldn't have been more than 35. Jack knew he shouldn't have been surprised. He'd learned during his Pentagon tour that many of the staffers on the Hill were twenty and thirty somethings generally infected with insatiable personal ambition, astounding arrogance and egocentric self-importance, and extraordinary ruthlessness in very large doses.

"As you know, I've been representing Brigadier General Emerson in connection with the Air Force inquiry into his performance as the Howard commander. As I suspect you also know, that report of investigation exonerated him in every pertinent detail."

"I haven't read the Salter report," replied the chief counsel coldly, "but I've got to tell you that I don't think it'll have a lot of traction with the members of the SASC, particularly since it's pretty clearly an example of the good old boy network in the Air Force protecting one of its own. General Upshaw's report raised substantial questions in the minds of several members regarding Emerson's fitness as an officer."

Undeterred, Kuhn continued. "In the interest of fair play, I wanted to share with you some research we've done into General Upshaw and his report. Are you aware of General Upshaw's recommendation regarding increased spending for high tech force protection systems?"

"Yes I am – so what?" answered Walker.

"Are you also aware that at the time he rendered that recommendation, he was also serving as a paid member of the board of directors of Riveson Corporation? And that Riveson Corporation has an entire division devoted to selling exactly the kinds of high-tech solutions Upshaw recommended DoD buy?"

"Go on," said Walker, suddenly looking both more interested and more uncomfortable.

"Are you also aware that at least two members of the SASC have close family members who own substantial amounts of Riveson stock?"

"What's your point," asked the chief counsel, now on the defensive.

Kuhn didn't flinch. "My point is this. You don't have to connect too many dots to conclude that Upshaw's findings are tainted, that he used his official position to promote the commercial interest of a company whose payroll he was on at the time he wrote his report. What better way to cultivate the market than to kill the career of some poor slob who hadn't been lucky enough to have the product Upshaw is selling. Throw in the fact that at least some SASC members have a similar economic interest in the financial prosperity of Riveson, and I think it's fair to say that you've got a fairly intriguing, and potentially fairly messy, news story."

"Is that your intention, to go public with this?" asked Walker.

"Only if justice requires it," answered Kuhn.

"What's your definition of justice?" asked the staff counsel, knowing full well by now what Kuhn had in mind.

"Justice will be served if General Emerson is confirmed for promotion to two-star rank. In such a case, I'd be willing to conclude that these obvious conflicts of interest were inadvertent and didn't improperly affect the outcome of this case."

"I understand," replied Walker. "If I can get you an answer by the end of the week, will that suffice for your purposes?"

"It will. By the way, I want to make it clear to both you and the SASC that General Emerson is not even aware of the information I've shared with you this morning."

"Noted," replied Walker, "that may actually make your proposed solution a bit easier."

"I thought it might. I'll leave my phone number with your receptionist," concluded Kuhn.

"Thank you for coming, Colonel. I'll be in touch."

As Kuhn walked out of the Hart Building to look for a cab back to Bolling, he had a good feeling. But he also knew it was probably a good thing that *his* name wouldn't be coming up to the SASC for confirmation anytime soon.

CHAPTER 26

Maxwell Air Force Base
Montgomery, Alabama
1100 hours, 14 September 2000

As he gazed idly out the window of his first-floor office at the vehicular and pedestrian traffic on "academic circle," Colonel Jack Kuhn reflected on his current lot in life, one he found most satisfactory.

Jack was now the Commandant, essentially the headmaster, of the USAF Judge Advocates School at the Air Force's education base in Montgomery. He didn't think he'd been the Judge Advocate General's first choice for the job, but when the Air Force Chief of Staff had asked him which assignment he'd like next, Kuhn had answered honestly. That's one thing about the military, Jack mused – *four stars always trump two stars.*

Kuhn turned back to the notes he was editing on his desk – he was scheduled to give a lecture on leadership right after lunch to the forty brand new judge advocates attending JASOC – the Judge Advocate Staff Officer Course – that was a prerequisite for all new Air Force military attorneys.

Jack really enjoyed his interaction with the shiny new JAG lieutenants who were just starting out on their own Air Force journeys - he found their youthful enthusiasm and bubbly zeal to be infectious. Jack also enjoyed the fact that he got to renew acquaintances with many of his old friends who came here for the various short courses his school taught in such diverse areas as labor law, environmental law, operations law, and advanced criminal practice. Jack guessed that virtually every one of the 950 uniformed attorneys in the Air Force would likely pass through his school during the course of his tour as commandant.

Satisfied that he had his stuff straight for the afternoon lecture, Kuhn glanced at his watch and saw that it was getting close to noon. As was happening more and more frequently these days, he had a lunch date.

Karen Babcock had been, and still was, the secretary for the colonel who ran the Air Force Chaplain's school, which occupied the other end of the Center for Professional Development building that also housed Jack's organization.

He'd noticed her in the hallway shortly after he took the reins of the JAG School a little over a year ago – they had first chatted a bit when he made a courtesy call appointment with his counterpart at the chaplain's school. She was an Alabama native who'd come home to Montgomery a few years ago after she and her husband of many years were divorced. Her only child, a son named Zach, Jack learned, had died of a rare childhood cancer many years ago when he was only three.

Jack had been smitten relatively quickly, he realized looking back, surprisingly captivated by her good looks, seemingly perpetual cheerfulness, and omnipresent smile. It had taken him a bit longer to do anything about it, however. He finally asked her out two months later as they talked over a cup of punch at the two schools' annual combined Christmas party.

Both still scarred by the dissolution of previous marriages, their relationship had developed slowly. Their innocuous first date - lunch at the Maxwell Officers Club - had been followed by another noontime meeting the following month, and another a month later.

By spring, though, Jack remembered, he and Karen had picked up the pace, "doing lunch" two or three times a week, and spending most Saturday evenings together, usually dinner and a movie. He'd finally popped the question a couple months ago. They'd talked about a big wedding, but it was Karen who pushed for a small civil ceremony . . . sooner rather than later. So it was that one month ago today, they'd spent their lunch hour at the courthouse in downtown Montgomery getting hitched by a justice of the peace.

Today, Jack and his wife would have lunch at one of his favorite places, a little eatery called "Tommy's" just outside the Day Street gate at Maxwell. Jack had been patronizing the little restaurant for well over two decades, ever since he and some of his classmates had discovered its cheap food and long neck beers when he was a new JAG student back in the fall of '74. Tommy's specialty was a concoction called Grecian spaghetti, which Kuhn invariably ordered – his only ordering decision was whether to get a full or a half order. Usually, he succumbed to his inner glutton and opted for the full order.

The restaurant didn't offer anything in the way of "upscale" atmosphere. Its booth seats, in fact, were covered with beat-up old vinyl, repaired in several spots with duct tape. And each booth had its own individual small metallic juke box of the sort that hadn't been chic since the '50s. That didn't matter much to Jack or to any of Tommy's other regular patrons - the food was good, the waitresses feisty but efficient, and two people could eat lunch there for under thirty dollars, a real rarity these days.

Karen was taking a day of leave today, and so had told Jack she'd meet him at the restaurant. Sure enough, she was already there when Jack walked in a little after noon.

"Hi, honey," she smiled, "having a good day?"

"It's been OK – just got better now, though," he smiled back.

"I took the liberty of ordering for you," Karen informed him.

"How'd you know what I want?" Jack replied with a twinkle in his eye.

"Duhh," Karen responded.

"Full order or half?" Jack inquired.

"Full, of course. I like my men to have some meat on their bones," she flirted.

Their salads appeared before Jack could think of a witty retort.

No matter how profoundly screwed up the rest of the world sometimes seemed to be, both Colonel and Mrs. Jack Kuhn continued to discover just how much they really liked being together, and so finished another wonderful lunch date. Then Jack was back to the base for his leadership lecture.

CHAPTER 27

Bolling Air Force Base
Washington, DC
1000 hours, 11 July 2001

Newly minted Brigadier General Wilkins didn't look anything like a flag officer this morning. Dressed in blue jeans and a tee shirt, he surveyed the large kitchen, cluttered with dozens of unopened boxes, of his newly assigned quarters on Westover Street, euphemistically known as "Generals' Row." He was glad he wouldn't have to do much unpacking himself – he was more than content to delegate those domestic duties to April.

Larry had met April six years ago on, of all things, a blind date orchestrated by General Buckingham, at the time the Deputy Judge Advocate General. Shortly thereafter, Buckingham got his second star and was appointed TJAG to replace the retiring Major General Elliott. Buckingham had always seemed to take a special interest in Larry and had counselled him on several occasions of the need for Larry to be married if he wanted to successfully compete for promotion to flag rank. April had turned out to be everything needed in a senior officer's wife – a classy native Bostonian who had been divorced ten years earlier, she came from money, was good looking and cultured, and was especially adept in social settings, which served her exceptionally well in her position as Deputy Chief of Protocol Services for the Department of Labor. She had one grown daughter, Penny, who was a sophomore at Radcliffe studying French literature. Already essentially a "finished project" with no further parental responsibility required on his part, she was to his way of thinking the ideal stepdaughter. Based on his own unhappily difficult childhood, Larry never had any desire to get involved in the child-rearing business – there were much more important things he wanted to do in life.

While Larry knew he wasn't "madly in love" with her, she was OK in the sack and seemed more than willing to put her own career on hold. And she never asked questions about how he spent his evenings whenever he was travelling (TDY) away from home.

Buckingham had been ecstatic when Larry told him of their engagement. Six months after they were married in 1994, in one of his first assignments as TJAG, Buckingham sent Larry to be the SJA at Ninth Air Force at Shaw AFB, South Carolina. That had turned out to be an easy gig, Larry recalled – Ninth Air Force was the Air Force component command with geographic responsibility for the Middle East, from which the U.S. was fortunately now largely disengaged ever since the Soviet-brokered Iraqi withdrawal from Kuwait. Plus, Larry had a terrific deputy, a go-getter lieutenant colonel named Bartlett, who did most of the heavy lifting when it came to handling that legal office's workload, including day-to-day management of the office's staff.

Less than two years later, when the incumbent SJA at Military Airlift Command (MAC) died from a sudden heart attack, General Buckingham called on Larry to move to Scott Air Force Base, Illinois, to take over the reins there. Again, Wilkins inherited a superb staff, which allowed him to take leadership credit for their work and focus on the legal needs of his boss, the four-star commander of MAC.

Finally, last year, General Buckingham had reassigned Larry as the Commander of the Air Force Legal Services Agency (AFLSA), with oversight over the judges, circuit prosecutors and defense attorneys, and a variety of other JAG offices performing various litigation and other functions in DC and elsewhere. It was the only job title in the entire JAG Corps that carried the word "commander"– several of the job's previous incumbents had been promoted to flag rank in past years. Wilkins was in that command position when Buckingham announced his pending retirement. His deputy, Brigadier General Cheryl

Connors, got her second star and was appointed to succeed Buckingham and become the next Judge Advocate General of the Air Force.

Although she was several years older than him and thus not a "competitor" with whom Larry ever concerned himself, he was not a fan of Connors, believing that her promotion had largely been the result of political correctness and affirmative action rather than merit. He had resolved, however, to be an effective deputy to her, particularly since she'd ultimately have a lot of sway when it was time for him to get his second star two or three years from now.

When the one-star board had met to select her successor as DJAG, Wilkins knew he was well positioned. Buckingham had written (actually, he had Larry draft it) an extremely effusive promotion recommendation form (PRF) that would be on the top of his personnel file to be reviewed by the promotion board. Along with the unqualified endorsement of the outgoing TJAG, Larry had built the right job history, including his meteoric rise over the past several years filling one important job after another.

Larry had liked his chances, but had known from his experience in the Career Management Office that there were two other very serious candidates for promotion that the Board would consider – Col Bernard Evers, the SJA at Strategic Air Command in Omaha, and Colonel Frank Rowe, the senior lawyer at Tactical Air Command at Langley AFB, VA. Both worked for powerful and influential four-star commanders who would no doubt push hard for each with their own strong promotion recommendations to the Board. Larry had known both men well for many years – he told others that he was not surprised when he heard that Evers, who Larry knew was something of a savant when it came to profanity, was accused of pervasive and offensive sexual harassment of the females in his office just before the board met, apparently as a result of an anonymous complainant. The Air Force Inspector General was required by law to inform the promotion board of the complaint and pending investigation, which effectively destroyed Evers' possibility for selection. Likewise, Rowe, who had a reputation for his temper, torpedoed his own candidacy several months before the board when a heated argument with his wife at their on-base house required security police intervention. That unfortunate incident was apparently the result of an unsigned letter he received alleging that his wife of many years was having an affair.

Wilkins had once thought that Jack Kuhn might also be a competitor standing in his way, but knew that he had effectively ensured during his Career Management gig that Kuhn would not be able to build a competitive resume in time to compete with him for promotion to BG. Larry knew that Kuhn could still be in the running, though, down the road. *That's ok*, Wilkins thought, *he might actually make a pretty good deputy for me when I get my second star in a couple years.*

Larry smiled as he recalled his euphoria when his selection had been announced. The Senate had confirmed his promotion last week, and his pin-on ceremony had taken place yesterday in the Pentagon. He was, without guilt, secretly happy that both his ne'er-do-well parents had passed away (Dad from a stroke, Mom in an auto accident) so many years ago, despite his pro forma remarks at the ceremony that he "so wished they could have been there to see their son promoted to flag rank." He much preferred to have his new trophy wife stand with him on this auspicious occasion rather than his mega-embarrassing mother and father.

Returning to his visual survey of his new cluttered kitchen, he looked at April in the next room – she had been a good choice, he congratulated himself. She'd get her first chance to accompany him on an official trip in a couple months. TJAG had told him just yesterday that he'd be traveling to the Soviet Union in September to represent the Air Force and JAG Corps at a big-deal legal conference being sponsored by the Ruskies as part of their expanding program of international military-military events. This one was designed to "promote the global respect for law and peace," at least according to their press release. General Connors' scheduled rotator cuff surgery scheduled for August would prevent her own attendance, she had told Larry. And because the conference schedule was rife with formal dinners and other protocol events, she told him that April was invited to go along on the trip at government expense.

Although Air Force officers seldom brought their spouses with them on official travel, this trip was an obvious exception given the many events at which a spouse's presence was almost obligatory. Given the fact that he was now recognizable by so many potentially prying eyes in DC, Wilkins had resolved not long ago to confine his personal "hunting" sessions almost exclusively to when he was TDY. Given that the upcoming Soviet conference would certainly involve the standard surreptitious surveillance of those in attendance by Russian intelligence services, this trip would obviously have to be a "no-hunting" zone for Larry, anyway – in other words, his wife's presence on this one would not "cramp his style." And there'd be a lot of other trips over the next several years without that annoying spousal constraint, he knew, subtly smiling at the thought.

CHAPTER 28

Brandenburg International Airport
Berlin, Germany
0900, September 11, 2001

Mohammed Atta had never really enjoyed flying. As the Soviet airliner lifted off the runway at Brandenburg Airport, it thus seemed ironic to him that Allah had decreed that Atta's personal path to Paradise should be via Aeroflot Flight 2463 from Berlin to Moscow.

Like the other five members of his team on the martyrdom mission, Atta knew this flight would be his last, as it would be, of course, for everybody else on board the half-full Russian airliner. Atta estimated that the number of empty seats was about the same as when he had taken the same flight two months earlier in preparation for the operation.

What Atta also knew, but the other Al Qaeda team members on board did not, was that this mission was but one of four being conducted this morning on order of Sheik Osama. Within a few hours, Atta thought with immense satisfaction, the godless Soviets will know the might of Allah's sword as none ever had. And he and his fellow soldiers of the Holy Jihad would soon know Allah's limitless beneficence and extraordinary pleasures in a glorious hereafter.

A Lufthansa jet which had left Frankfurt International Airport about 45 minutes ago, and two flights which had already departed from King Khaled International Airport in Riyadh, Saudi, Arabia, also carried Al Qaeda martyrdom teams, Atta knew. In some ways, he wished that he could be on the Saudia flight to Moscow. That flight carried in its cargo hold a steamer trunk containing a very carefully crafted weapon that employed a powerful explosive imbedded in a package of radioactive material obtained from Bin Laden's Iranian sources. When it was detonated just before impact in the financial district of Moscow, the deadly low altitude airburst would provide a truly spectacular demonstration of the awesome power of Allah's warriors.

It would also preoccupy the Soviet authorities and emergency response teams, diverting their attention from the two targets within the Kremlin walls that would be struck within the following sixty minutes.

Given the extensive network Al Qaeda now had at its disposal within the Kingdom of Saudi Arabia, it had not been difficult to arrange to get the trunk through King Khaled's lax security apparatus and onto the plane. Nor would the martyrs aboard each of the two Saudia flights – the other did not carry a bomb and was bound for Kabul – arouse any suspicion on aircraft whose passenger lists already consisted largely of Arab males.

No, he had been right to decide to personally command the more difficult German operations. Atta had lived in the Deutsch Republic off and on during the past four years and knew both German airports extremely well – he'd flown in and out of them more than three dozen times.

While neither the German nor Soviet aircraft carried any explosive weapon – German baggage security was simply too difficult to circumvent – the planes themselves would be the weapons. Despite the length of the journeys, the Sheik's technical experts had determined that there would be sufficient fuel left in the tanks to accentuate the desired death and damage at the two adjacent targets within the huge Kremlin compound. His cousin Marwan Al-Shehhi's plane would slam into the Supreme Soviet building about 15 minutes before Atta's aircraft impacted into the southwest side of the Soviet "Senate" building. Atta's target, he knew, housed both the living quarters and executive office of the infidel Putin himself.

Atta supposed that when Soviet investigators determined that both he and Marwan had received flight training in Florida, as well as Hani Hanjour who would be taking the controls of the flight to Kabul and Ahmed Alhaznawi who would pilot the Saudia airliner containing the dirty bomb, they would suspect U.S. complicity in the attacks. That was fine with Atta - he hated American decadence almost as much as he hated the Soviets, who had inflicted so much pain and suffering on the faithful within their own borders and in so many other countries as well. His hatred of the USSR was further amplified by the infuriating knowledge that so many thousands of its military advisors were now stationed in the Kingdom of Saudi Arabia, and that they were there with the full consent and complicity of the corrupt royals. It was as vile a desecration as Atta could imagine, an unforgivable breach by the House of Saud of its sacred duty to serve as the protector of the Holy Cities of Mecca and Medina.

Some ninety minutes later, the Aeroflot pilot announced in both Russian and German that the aircraft was about 400 kilometers from Moscow, and that it would arrive as scheduled in less than an hour. That fortuitous announcement confirmed Atta's own assessment of where they were.

It was time.

From his seat at the front of first class, Atta stood up and stepped into the aisle. His fellow martyr Wail Alshehri, who had occupied the window seat next to him, followed Atta into the aisle and walked back to the curtain that separated first class from coach. Seeing Alshehri open the curtain, the four other martyrs, all of whom had been seated in aisle seats in coach, stood up and moved rapidly to the front of the airplane. Each had a box cutter clutched in his right hand, razors now extended and protruding several centimeters from their handles.

A male flight attendant confronted them at about row 12, telling them forcefully in both German and Russian that they must sit down. He was rewarded with what he first thought was a fist to his stomach

– it wasn't until he tried to get up from the aisle floor that he noticed both the blood on his shirt and the sharp pain of the stab wound.

Speaking in German which he knew and then in a Russian phrase he had memorized, Atta announced that the plane was being hijacked, but that if the passengers and flight attendants cooperated and did not resist, no one else would be hurt. Working quickly, the team herded them all to the rear of the cabin. Three of the martyrs then moved to the front of the coach section to stand watch over their captives while a fourth, Wail's brother Waleed, joined Atta and Alshehri in the now empty first-class section, closing the curtain behind him.

Atta opened the unlocked cockpit door and repeated the hijack announcement to the two-man flight crew in the Russian he had rehearsed. He also told the captain in another memorized phrase to come immediately into the passenger cabin to hear the hijacker's terms. The Russian left-seater, thoroughly trained in current hijack response doctrine which mandated a "cooperate and survive" approach, complied and left his co-pilot to fly the airliner.

The Alshehri brothers sat the captain in Row 3 and told him to be quiet, tying his hands and feet with twine that Atta had in his briefcase in the bin above where he had been seated for most of the flight. Meanwhile, Atta took the empty left seat in the cockpit, using yet another Russian phrase to tell the copilot that he would shortly be providing him new vector instructions. The co-pilot, also fully versed on hijack doctrine, nodded assent.

Looking forward at his instruments, the co-pilot never saw Waleed approach from behind a minute later. The elder Alshehri expertly jerked the co-pilot's head back by his hair with his left hand and quickly slit his throat with the box cutter in his right. The co-pilot's body was then dragged out of the cockpit, and laid in the row just in front of the one where his pilot, who had been similarly executed by Wail only seconds earlier, now lay.

The first thing Atta did was to turn off the aircraft's transponder. That having been accomplished, he checked his altimeter and compass – the aircraft was at 10,000 meters as it should be and still vectored due east. Everything was in order, *praise be to Allah*.

He estimated that he was now less than 300 kilometers from Moscow. The weather over this part of the Soviet Union was reasonably clear as he knew it would be – had the weather reports and satellite imagery on the internet last night not indicated VFR conditions in the target area, of course, the missions would have had to be aborted.

He looked straight ahead out of the cockpit window at the horizon, straining to see the initial indication of the skyline of the huge city he knew lay ahead. He was still searching two minutes later when he first noticed the rapidly enlarging plume of dirty black smoke rising in the far distance about 15 degrees to his left.

Allah is great, thought Atta with an incredible rush of happiness. The Saudia flight had accomplished its mission, he proudly knew.

Atta estimated he was now less than thirty minutes from his target, and vectored the aircraft toward the growing plume that would now serve as his approach beacon.

The fifty-five passengers on Flight 2463 had been herded to the rear of the aircraft when Atta and his team had taken control of the flight. Among those passengers were Brigadier General Larry Wilkins, travelling in civilian clothes as per regulation, his wife, and Anna Kasparov, a Department of Defense translator who had been assigned to this trip to assist Wilkins. The three of them were currently in the left three seats of row 33. There were four other young American students, two men and two women, who also among those crowded in rows 25 through 35 - the rest of the airborne hostages were mostly Russian males.

Fortuitously, Larry had attended the flag officers' anti-terrorism course, mandatory for all new general officers, only a month earlier. He clearly remembered the unequivocal instruction the attendees received

. . . since virtually all hijackings, based on an unbroken history over the past half century, have ultimately been peacefully resolved, the correct approach for a high-value passenger such as himself was to keep a very low profile and do nothing to antagonize the hijackers. As per his recent training, he had already surreptitiously removed his military ID from his wallet and slipped it to the bottom of the seat pocket in front of him.

Two rows in front of him, one of the Russian passengers, a large man who appeared to be in his early 40s, was talking almost in a whisper on a cell phone. He appeared to lose the connection to whoever he was talking to after less than 60 seconds. He then turned to the male passenger next to him and began a conversation in Russian.

"What's he saying?" Larry asked Kasparov.

"He said he was talking to his wife who lives in Leningrad. She says two hijacked airplanes crashed into Moscow this morning."

That unsettled Wilkins, who had been working hard to maintain a cool demeanor - he had allowed himself to muse over the past few minutes about how he could use his involvement in this hijacking to his professional advantage after it was over, particularly when it came to his long-term ambition to enter politics after he retired from the Air Force as TJAG. That's where the real power, perks, and money were, he knew. *Voters love heroes*, he also knew.

The big Russian kept talking to his seatmate and Kasparov continued to translate for Larry.

"He says we've got to take back control of this airplane before we crash too. He also says he used to fly airplanes when he was younger and can fly this one. He says we out-number these fucking Arabs ten to one. He says all the men need to go forward together with him and kill the rotten bastards." Several of the Russians in the rows ahead seemed to be quietly relaying the big Russian's message to each other, and Larry saw some of them men slightly nodding approval.

Larry was struck with a sudden wave of fear on hearing his translator's words, but tried hard to maintain a cool demeanor, while his wife, on the other hand, started sobbing uncontrollably, albeit quietly, leaning in toward Larry. Wilkins was in no mood to be sympathetic or supportive right now, and told her angrily in a low voice, "Cut that shit out right now, god damnit – I've got to think!" and pushed her roughly away from him.

While the Russians in the rows ahead of them were furtively planning their assault, Larry pulled out his government Blackberry out of his pocket and sent a short text to General Connors and to his secretary back in the Pentagon. *Am on hijacked plane - am organizing attack to retake control*, the text read. He hoped it would go through.

Five minutes later, the big Russian stood up and spoke the Russian phrase for "let's go." Over twenty Russian males and the two male American students rose from their seats as one and started moving en masse toward the front of the plane. Larry waited to get up and move forward until the group of male passengers was well down the aisle, almost to the curtain dividing first class from coach where two of the startled hijackers stood. Once in the aisle, he could see and hear the melee that had already begun. As he carefully walked forward toward the mass of combatants, he thought of himself as a chess master sacrificing his pawns in the initial advance. That's the right play, he concluded – *that's what Caesar would do.*

In the cockpit, Atta had descended to 4,000 meters and the huge city was now plainly in view less than sixty kilometers ahead. His heart leapt again when he saw a second smaller plume begin to rise to the right of the first, which had flattened and grown less dark as it continued to expand. His cousin was now in Paradise, he thought with enormous satisfaction. Atta knew he would be joining him shortly.

So fixated was Atta by the glorious sights ahead that he didn't at first hear the shouting and commotion in the cabin behind him. Less than ten seconds after he heard Waleed's startled shriek, the door to the cockpit came crashing in and he was suddenly struck in the head by one of the three big men – they were Russian based on their frenzied epithets - who were now attempting to wrestle him out of his seat. Atta grappled mightily with his attackers in the tiny cockpit until he was suddenly pulled to his right and felt the excruciating pain of a box cutter's blade piercing his left shoulder. Then another burning stab ripped at the back at his neck just below his left ear, followed by yet another that sliced his cheek. As the viciously painful pummeling continued unabated and drove him to the brink of unconsciousness, he distinctly experienced a surprising feeling of weightlessness, almost as if the airplane had suddenly gone into a steep vertical dive. It was the last sentient feeling Mohammed Atta would ever have in this life.

CHAPTER 29

Maxwell Air Force Base
Montgomery, Alabama
1100 hours, 13 September 2001

As he sipped his fourth cup of coffee this particular morning, Colonel Jack Kuhn sat at his desk reflecting on the astounding events of the past two days.

Something triggered a synapse, and Jack reminded himself that he needed to draft a reply to the nice letter he'd received last week from his old client Steve Emerson, now a three-star general, who had written him to personally recommend a young JAG who wanted to join Kuhn's faculty at the JAG School.

Of course, with the extraordinary events of earlier this week, Jack thought he probably wouldn't be faulted for a tardy reply. The TV in Jack's office was turned on to CNN, as it had been almost non-stop since Tuesday morning.

Like everyone else in country, Jack had wakened Tuesday to the news of the devastating terrorist attack on the Soviet Union. Though not yet absolutely certain, it was looking very much like Muslim terrorists, probably part of the Al Qaeda organization, were behind the very well-orchestrated attacks on Moscow and the Soviet embassy in Afghanistan.

Jack remembered vividly the CNN video replay of the giant black plume rising over the Moscow city center where the Saudi airplane had just crashed. Then, incredibly, he and the rest of the world watched in horror as the CNN cameraman quickly jerked his camera upward to catch a glimpse of the hijacked Lufthansa airliner diving down into the Kremlin. Although there had been no similar video of the Saudi airplane striking the Soviet embassy in Kabul, its devastating result had likewise been fully documented on TV screens around the planet.

There had also been one other flight hijacked that day, an Aeroflot jet from Germany, but it had crashed under mysterious circumstances into a farmer's field about 20 miles outside the Soviet capital. Apparently, there had been a number of Americans on that flight, though their identities had not yet been released to the public by Aeroflot authorities.

There was considerable current speculation in the media suggesting that the airliner had been shot down by a MIG fighter before it reached its intended destination, although the Soviets were not commenting on that possibility. What the doomed Aeroflot flight's intended terror destination had been was also a subject of non-stop discussion on all the news networks.

The initial death count of the concerted terrorist attack was truly staggering – over 4,000 dead in Moscow and another 900 or so in Afghanistan. That the toll would likely go much higher hadn't been obvious until later on Tuesday, when a Soviet spokesman soberly announced that the Saudi flight had apparently carried a "dirty bomb" which scattered deadly radioactive waste over an area of several square kilometers of the city. It now appeared that an additional 50,000 people in the affected area were at very significant risk of dying from radiation poisoning.

Kuhn thought that Soviet Premier Putin had been remarkably composed when he addressed his people and the world several hours after the attack, particularly since Putin had very nearly been a casualty himself. The German airliner had struck and demolished the Supreme Soviet Building right next door to another large structure that housed Putin's office and residence. That building, called the "Senate" (Jack had had no idea the Soviets had a building called the Senate) was moderately damaged by flying debris, but the ensuing fire that consumed the portion of Supreme Soviet building that hadn't been demolished on impact had not reached its next-door neighbor. Remarkably, Putin hadn't been injured.

Putin's brief address had, of course, articulated his outrage and unmistakably signaled that there would be retribution. Of that, Jack had no doubt – clearly more people were going to die before this was all over, and Jack suspected that neither the United States nor any other nation on Earth, with one likely exception, would protest when the Soviets responded militarily as they inevitably would. America was also, Jack knew, at the forefront of the many nations now flying in relief and medical supplies to the USSR.

All of the twenty or so hijackers had, of course, been killed along with their victims. At least they received proportionate justice, Jack thought, contrasting their fate to that of the American Nazi wacko who killed so many people in Oklahoma City back in '95. The Supreme Court's highly controversial decision last session declaring the death penalty an unconstitutionally "cruel and unusual" punishment had spared the undeserving O'Neil's life, Jack knew, along with everyone else sitting on death rows throughout the country.

Although Al Qaeda had not publicly claimed credit for the horrific attack on Russia, there seemed little doubt that responsibility lay with Osama Bin Laden and his growing network of Islamic terrorists. Based on the intel report that Jack had listened to at the Air University commander's Wednesday morning staff meeting, Bin Laden was likely hiding at one his several camps in mountainous eastern Iran near the Afghanistan border.

Jack noticed that CNN was currently covering the emergency session of the UN Security Council, where the Soviet ambassador had just publicly demanded that Iran turn over Bin Laden and other Al Qaeda leaders. The Iranian ambassador was speaking now, emphatically denying that Bin Laden or any member of Al Qaeda was within his country's borders. More to come, thought Jack.

Hitting the mute button on his remote, Jack turned back to the notes he was editing on his desk – he was scheduled to give a lecture to the Air War College this afternoon on the law of armed conflict. Pretty timely, he thought wryly.

Satisfied that he had his stuff straight for the afternoon lecture, Kuhn glanced at his watch and saw that it was getting close to noon. On schedule, his wife walked into his office with a brown paper bag containing a sandwich for each of them and a couple of diet cokes.

"Hi, honey," she smiled, "having a good day?"

"It's been OK – just got better now," he smiled back.

"Isn't it awful what happened in Russia?" asked Karen, just before taking the first bite of her salad.

"Freaking incredible," answered Jack. "There's no way I would have thought Bin Laden could pull off something so sophisticated."

"You think he did it?" asked Karen.

"I'd bet an awful lot of money on it," Jack offered.

"What do you think the Russians are going to do?" Karen continued her questioning.

"I think they'll go after Al Qaeda with everything they've got. And they've got a lot," opined the JAG.

"It's not going to be pretty, is it?"

"Nope. I don't think the Soviets will be looking to take a lot of prisoners," Jack agreed.

"When do you think it'll happen," Karen asked.

"I think it's probably already happening, at least with the KGB. I won't be surprised, though, if the Soviets don't do something major militarily before the end of the year," Jack responded.

"Very strange times," said Karen, "I'm just glad those fanatics didn't come after us."

"Amen," said Jack.

After that, they agreed to discuss something a bit less depressing while they ate. As they were finishing up their low-budget lunch date,

Jack's secretary burst into the office, visibly close to tears. Without being asked, she blurted, "Awful news, sir. TJAG just sent a message that General Wilkins and his wife were on board the hijacked flight that crashed in Russia."

CHAPTER 30

The White House, Washington DC
9:30 a.m., January 2, 2002

President Al Gore strode into the surprisingly small White House Situation Room looking like a man with a lot on his mind. Vice President Joe Lieberman was already at his assigned place at the table, and like everyone else in the room, rose when the President entered.

"Okay, folks, let's get down to it," commanded Gore.

The briefer at the podium was Air Force General Richard Kinego, the current Chairman of the Joint Chiefs of Staff.

"Good morning, Mr. President," started Kinego, "my purpose is to give you a detailed update regarding the current military situation in Iran." A large map of Iran came up on the screen behind the Chairman.

"As you know, last week Tehran formally refused to comply with what Putin said was his final ultimatum to turn over Osama Bin Laden and a number of other known terrorists. The JCS counsel tells me that Putin was on solid legal ground under international law, since U.N. Security Council Resolution 917 calls for Iran to surrender anyone suspected of complicity in the 9-11 attacks.

"As a result of the Iranian refusal, yesterday the Soviet Union and Iraq began sustained military operations clearly aimed both at taking down the government in Tehran and directly attacking Al Qaeda strongholds."

"Let me interrupt here, General," interjected the President, "I was advised just last week by the CIA that the Iranians were likely to give up Bin Laden to the Russians. What's your take on what happened?"

"Sir," responded Kinego, "our intel folks indicate that a sizable moderate element within the Iranian government wanted to do exactly that. We also know, however, that some powerful hardline clerics in the government violently opposed any such accommodation. It seems clear that the hard-liners won out."

"That brilliant decision will probably cost them their country," offered the President.

"You're almost certainly correct, Mr. President," answered Kinego. "As I was saying, the Soviets and Iraqis are executing a very coordinated battle plan."

"By the way, General, do you have any idea why Iran ever allowed Bin Laden to establish such a toehold in their country in the first place?" asked the President. "I thought Shia Muslims like the Iranians hated Sunni Muslims like Bin Laden."

"As a general proposition you are correct, Sir," responded the Chairman. "But I think their alliance is simply an example of the old war maxim that 'the enemy of my enemy is my friend.' Apparently, both the Shias and the Sunnis appear to hate the Soviets more than they hate each other these days."

"That makes as much sense as any theory I've heard on the subject," replied Gore. "Please continue."

Turning to the map behind him, Kinego pointed to the lower left-hand corner. "Three Iraqi Republican Guard divisions crossed the border in a classic tank blitzkrieg to roll over Iranian defenses and take the southwest corner of Iran all the way to Zagros Mountains. They've forcibly occupied four major cities – Khorramshahr, Abadan, Ahvaz, and Dezfel – on the way. Although they've now paused, the Iraqis now control the major Iranian oil fields in that region. Iraqi MIGs also conducted a very effective air attack on Bandar e-Bushehr on the Persian Gulf coast well south of their main attack. That air raid appears to have taken down the robust Iranian anti-air and anti-shipping systems that were positioned there."

"How about the big Iranian base near the Strait of Hormuz," interrupted the President, using his laser pointer to highlight the narrow choke point between Oman and Iran.

"You're referring to Bandar e-Abbas, Mr. President. Thus far, our imagery shows no attack on that base, but it's logical to assume that either the Soviets or the Iraqis have it on their target list. I'd guess the Soviets will work that target using carrier-based assets – it'd be a long reach for Iraqi MIGs," responded Kinego, waving his pointer over the map to demonstrate the 700-mile distance between Iraq's nearest air base and the potential Iranian target.

Kinego raised his eyes and his pointer upward to the upper left had corner of the map on the screen. "While the Iraqis were moving down south, a Soviet armored force of about 50,000 crossed into Iran from the Soviet Republic of Azerbaijan. They've already taken Ardabil, just across the border, and are now moving quickly toward Tabriz. We estimate that they'll be able to eliminate Iranian resistance there within forty-eight hours."

"And if they take Tabriz, they'll have a straight corridor southeast to Tehran?" Gore asked.

"Correct, sir," answered the Chairman "though it will no doubt take at least a couple of weeks to move a force that size to Tehran."

"Meanwhile," continued Kinego, "Three armored Soviet divisions were simultaneously crossing the border from Turkmenistan near the Caspian. They've already taken Gonbad e-Kavos," said Kinego, moving his pointer to the upper right corner of the map to pinpoint that Iranian city. "From there, they'll be in a position to drive south and isolate the eastern third of the country."

"That's where they think Bin Laden is?" asked Gore.

"Yes sir, they do. So do we."

"What else do you have General?" prompted the President.

"There are three other major pieces to the offensive, Mr. President," answered the JCS Chairman. "First is a strategic bombing campaign that is already well underway targeting communications nodes and anti-aircraft systems throughout the country, including Tehran." Kinego tapped his pointer at several locations on the map.

"There's also a naval component to this conflict," continued Kinego.

"Don't the Iranians have submarines?" asked the President.

"Yes sir," answered the Chairman. "They've got two attack subs they bought from the Chinese. One is currently in port, the other put out to sea a week ago and is likely somewhere in the Gulf of Oman."

"And the Russian navy?" asked Gore.

"They've got two carriers nearby in the Indian Ocean already conducting flight operations. Like our Navy, the Russians employ a good-sized battle group to protect their carriers, so I think it's unlikely that a single Iranian sub poses much threat to either Soviet flattop. I think it more likely that that the Iranian can is running like hell trying to stay away from the five or six Soviet subs that are trying to track it down as we speak."

"In other words," said the President, "you wouldn't want to sell life insurance to the Iranian submariners."

"No sir," responded the Chairman with a short grin. "The final offensive element is a special operations campaign designed to take down or seize specific high value targets, including some of the known Al Qaeda camps and potentially Bin Laden himself. We don't have a great deal of intelligence yet on the specifics of those operations, but we know they're going on. Both Pakistan and Afghanistan have closed their borders with Iran and moved a sizeable number of troops to their respective frontiers to enforce that closure. Although we don't expect the Pakis or the Afghans to actively participate in this war, it's clear that they're cooperating with the Russians to the extent that appear to be attempting to cut off any escape route for Bin Laden to the east."

"What have losses been like so far?" asked Gore.

"Obviously hard to tell with certainty at this point, sir. We know that the Soviets have already lost four or five MIGs to SAMs. The Iranian Air Force has lost about two dozen jets in the air, and a lot more on the ground."

"Spoken like a true flyboy, Dick," smiled the President, "how about *human* casualties?"

"I was about to get to that Mr. President, honestly," Kinego sheepishly smiled, causing a brief ripple of nervous laughter around the table. "Our best guess is that Soviet personnel losses during the first day are less than two hundred KIA. We think the Iraqis may have lost about three hundred, mostly infantry troops, taking Ahvaz and probably another couple hundred or so in their other engagements. We think Iranian casualties are much higher, probably in the neighborhood of 5,000 KIA to this point."

"What's your bottom-line military assessment?" asked the President.

"It's the Pentagon consensus that the Soviets can take down the Iranian government in six to eight weeks, maybe sooner if some Iranian opposition groups coalesce effectively. The occupation part may be the long pole in the tent. Iran is an awfully big country with a lot of people, something close to 70 million. And some significant hard-core percentage of that population is likely to be anxious to take an early train to Paradise if they can dispatch some Russian infidels in the process. As to when the Soviets might get Bin Laden or his key lieutenants, it's anybody's guess – those mountains that run the length of Iran in the east are a very tough environment to fight in and offer a lot of real good hiding places."

"One final question, General, is there any possibility of this thing going nuke?" asked the President.

"Is there a possibility, yes," answered Kinego, "is there a likelihood, no. We don't think Iran has more than a half dozen weapons, and they probably don't have any reliable means to deliver them outside their own border, particularly now that the Russians are taking apart the Iranian Air Force. Plus, they know Saddam has about two dozen nukes, and would love an excuse to try to turn Tehran into a parking lot. We're convinced that absent any Iranian first use, the Soviets will bend over backwards to keep this from going nuclear."

"That's my assessment as well, General," responded the President. "Thank you for an excellent briefing."

"Let me share with you in this room some additional information," continued Gore. "As a few of you already know, I received a heads-up call on New Year's Eve from Vladimir Putin informing me that the Soviets would be moving on Iran within 24 hours. I told him that I understood, and urged him to do everything possible to keep hostilities from going nuclear. He assured me that he totally agreed, and said that he's made it clear to his generals, and to Saddam as well, that there will be no use of Soviet or Iraqi nuclear weapons, or any other WMD for that matter, without Putin's personal approval. I believe him."

The President went on. "Putin also volunteered that he has made it absolutely clear to the Iraqis that under no circumstances will they make any move against Israel. Of course, our friend Itzhak has about four times as many nukes as Saddam, and you military guys have told me that their Jericho is a much better delivery system than the Scud. Based on that and what Putin said, I'm satisfied that Israel likely won't be dragged into this one."

All those around the table nodded silent approval of that welcome assessment.

The President concluded, "All right everybody, we know this isn't our fight. God knows we've got enough problems to keep us busy here at home. But I want to stay at DEFCON 4 while this is going on just to be on the safe side. Let's continue to find out everything we can, and arrange to get me current intelligence updates first thing every morning and then again around quitting time. Are there any questions?"

There being none, President Gore got up and headed back to the Oval Office.

EPILOGUE

The Pentagon
Arlington, Virginia
0800, 31 March 2009

As he walked into his office suite on the fourth floor of the Pentagon this day, Major General Jack Kuhn couldn't believe his military career was almost over. He also couldn't believe he was actually retiring as The Judge Advocate General of the Air Force.

He cast a glance, as he always did when he entered the suite, at the bust of his old friend Larry Wilkins sitting on a prominent five-foot pedestal at the rear of the larger outer office where execs and secretaries had their desks. The bust had been presented to the Air Force with a great deal of fanfare at a White House ceremony several years ago by the Soviet Ambassador to the U.S. – the plaque at its base simply read "Brigadier General Lawrence A. Wilkins – Honored Hero of the of the Soviet Union." Jack had attended that presentation ceremony, remembering the ambassador's effusive narrative describing how Larry had so gallantly partnered with fellow passenger Igor Rozhkov to lead the counterattack that prevented the Islamic terrorists from reaching Moscow, thus thwarting their evil mission.

The last seven years had been truly extraordinary. After Larry Wilkin's death fighting the 911 terrorists, Major General Connors, at that point the only flag officer in the Corps, had quickly reassigned him in early 2002 from the JAG School back to the Pentagon to serve as her acting deputy, even though he was still a colonel. Jack had always been a fan of Cheryl Connors, who had a long-standing reputation as a dynamo "commander's lawyer" who always seemed to get the best out of those who worked for her. He concluded after only a few weeks working for her that her sterling reputation was not only well-deserved, but actually understated. He very much enjoyed working for her . . . and learned a lot.

The one-star promotion board that met less than a year later, based largely on Connors very strong push, had promoted Jack to brigadier general and the "Acting" portion of his job title was removed. Two and a half years later, Jack had been promoted again, and became Connors' successor as TJAG when she retired in 2005. Kuhn knew the fact that his former client Steve Emerson was by then a four-star and Chief of Staff of the Air Force no doubt had a lot to do with Jack's quick ascent to the top of the JAG Corps.

Jack entered his private office and sat down at his desk, for the last time as an active-duty officer. His desk was uncharacteristically uncluttered – Jack had come in last Sunday to completely empty his in-basket and box up his personal papers and effects. Karen, four-year-old Jack Jr., and Heather and her husband Rob wouldn't be here for another half hour.

It's been a hell of a career, he reminisced, thinking back to the naïve young go-getter he'd been when he'd come on board fresh out of law school in 1974. *Older, and a good bit wiser*, he was pretty sure.

It was sure not the same world as when he'd first put on a uniform, he knew with certainty. For starters, back then there had been some sense of global balance, with America and the Soviet Union roughly equal military adversaries. That served to prevent either side from doing anything really silly for a lot of years.

The America of today, Jack knew sadly, was nowhere near the military equal of the USSR, or even the Chinese – not a shocker, thought Jack, when a country devotes less than 10% of its budget to defense. His own piece of the pie – the entire Air Force JAG Corps – was now only about 60% of the size it had been, and had lost two of its four general officer positions during the draconian drawdown of the early 90s. He was nevertheless extremely proud of the terrific work his reduced collection of lawyers and paralegals had done and continued to do, frequently under difficult conditions, during his watch as TJAG.

Kuhn knew, of course, that there was a limitless list of critical domestic needs that the government needed to spend its money on – social security, Medicare, homelessness, dealing with rampant crime and drug abuse, and funding the scores of federal work projects designed to put as many folks as possible back to work, to name but a few. And the inevitable oil shock that had followed the outbreak of hostilities in the Middle East hadn't helped America a bit – Jack remembered everyone's dismay when gas prices first broke the five-dollar barrier last year. Sometimes Kuhn actually sympathized with the politicians and their impossible jobs of trying to find enough dollars to meet all the country's many needs.

Of course, things weren't all light and roses for the mighty Soviet Union either, Jack knew. They'd lost a lot of troops overthrowing the ayatollahs in Iran, and were still hemorrhaging human life at a scary rate as they continued, after all these years, to struggle to pacify the country they'd conquered. There were actually beginning to be, at least according to the media, serious rumblings of discontent within the USSR, whose economy was now beginning to buckle under the strain of their hugely expensive Global War on Terrorism, which also seemed to be consistently generating at least fifty new Russian widows and sets of grieving parents every week.

There was also growing indication, Jack knew, of previously unthinkable grumbling on the part of several of the USSR's eastern European allies, who were being called upon to provide huge amounts of money and considerable numbers of troops to conduct the never-ending "peacekeeping" operations in Iran.

And try as they might, the Soviets still hadn't been able to get Bin Laden. Their relentless chase had put him on the defensive, of course, and there had been no further attacks on the scale of 9-11. But Osama was still out there somewhere. Every day he remained unkilled or uncaptured seemed to increase his status as a folk hero among so many of the "faithful" and the dispossessed in the Middle East, who were increasingly relying upon his inspiration to foment further trouble for the Soviets and their supporters in the region.

The recent Ramadan riots in Mecca, Jeddah, and Riyadh were but one example, Jack knew. The coordinated mob actions unmistakably bore Al Qaeda fingerprints and resulted in more than a thousand dead, including a few minor Royals. The once invulnerable House of Saud had, in fact, teetered on the brink for over several days until the demonstrations were finally brutally put down by loyalist forces - the beheadings of the nearly one hundred accused perpetrators who had been captured went on for weeks afterward. The Saudi government had hung on by their fingernails, but no one was now betting much on their long-term survival.

Iraq wasn't in much better shape, Jack knew. They'd lost 20,000 troops, and a hell of a lot of tanks and artillery pieces, one month into the war seven years ago when the crazy cleric ordered the launch of an Iranian nuclear Scud at an Iraqi staging point outside of Atak. The Iraqis had massed there in preparation for a final two hundred mile push up to Tehran to join the Soviets, who were already laying siege to the city from the northeast. Iraq's retaliatory nuclear strike on the city of Esfahan had killed five times as many Iranians, though most of them had been civilians.

The Soviets had, thank God, been able to regain control of the situation, and those had been the only two nukes unleashed during the war. But guerrilla-style revenge attacks on Iraqis in the southwest corner of Iran they now occupied continued unabated, clearly a very passionate pursuit for a good many Persians.

No, thought Kuhn, *things aren't going all that well for the Soviet Union, either*. Being the world's undisputed superpower didn't appear to him to be all that good a deal.

Some minutes later, Karen and Jackie arrived and were escorted into Kuhn's office, and sat down on the couch facing his desk. Much to Jack's surprise, literally seconds later, retired four-star general Mick Casey walked in unannounced. Jack had invited him to the retirement ceremony, but didn't think the demands of Casey's current job, Executive Vice President of defense industry giant United Aerospace, would permit him to attend. Casey was dressed in the three-piece suit that was his current uniform these days - it was a wonderful if abbreviated visit. He'd not met Karen before, and seemed genuinely impressed with her. And he hadn't seen Heather since she was a little girl - he thoughtfully made a big deal about what a terrific young lady she had grown up to be. He then excused himself as quickly as he had come, after telling Jack he wanted to have lunch with him next week to talk about his future.

At ten minutes to nine, CSAF's protocol officer arrived at Kuhn's office to escort him and his family to the retirement ceremony. She gave all of them a quick down and dirty briefing while they walked regarding the details and sequence of events for the imminent ceremony, soon arriving at a small office known as the "Green Room" adjacent to the auditorium where the ceremony would be held. Five minutes later, CSAF's exec knocked on the door, and advised them it was time to begin. This was suddenly all happening very fast, Jack thought.

Jack was surprised at how many people had shown up – he estimated that there were over three hundred folks crowded in the room. After the tape-recorded Ruffles and Flourishes and the playing of the national anthem, at which everyone stood at attention, General Emerson entered and asked everyone, including Jack, to sit down. Emerson spent the next ten minutes describing, entirely without notes, Jack's entire career. The Chief effusively highlighted his two SJA tours, his performance during Operation Just Cause during which he won the bronze star, his work as a chief circuit defense counsel, how Jack had so brilliantly represented him in his own time of legal need, the work that

Jack had done as commandant of the JAG School, and most recently his amazing work in the Pentagon leading the entire JAG Corps. Jack found General Emerson's unabashed praise a little embarrassing. After winding up his remarks, CSAF invited everyone to rise. The narrator then read an equally laudatory award citation, and Emerson pinned a Defense Superior Service medal on Jack's chest. Then the narrator read the brief retirement order, and Jack was offered the floor.

Jack had thought about what he ought to say, of course, but had opted not to script his comments. He thanked General Emerson for officiating, thanked several people attending the ceremony for their presence, including especially retired CSAF Casey.

Then Jack got to what he knew would be the harder part. He talked about Karen, of course, and how important she had been to him. He started to lose his composure when he talked about Heather, and how proud he was to be her father. He finally did lose his composure, albeit briefly, when he told the audience that he was sure his other daughter Cindy was looking down on the proceedings from heaven. Many in the crowd lost their own composure when, after he presented floral bouquets to Karen and Heather, he held up a third bouquet above his head, looked up, expressed his love and told Cindy that these were for her.

It took him several seconds after that to finish his impromptu speech. He wiped his eyes and pressed on, describing what an honor it had been to serve, and how much he would miss the Air Force and the camaraderie of those he served with. He repeated an all-encompassing thank you, snapped an unscheduled last salute to General Emerson, and the speech was over. It took another fifteen minutes for him to shake hands and/or hug – as appropriate – each of the attendees as they moved through the obligatory receiving line.

When he'd shaken the last hand, Jack felt physically exhausted. There were now just the five of them – Jack, Karen, Jackie, Heather and her husband – left in the big room. Karen and Heather both embraced

Jack for several long seconds, and he sniffled a little more. "Damn, that was hard," he said to his wife.

"I could tell," replied his wife with a smile that was both impish and caring. "Really, Jack," she said, "you couldn't have been better."

The five of them walked out of the auditorium, turning right to head to the Pentagon's Executive Dining Room for a luncheon in his honor. Although neither Emerson nor Casey would be able to attend this follow-on celebration, virtually all other attendees would be there.

They walked down a stairwell to the third floor, then turned right from the E-Ring when they reached the Tenth Corridor. They arrived at the Dining Room two minutes later.

Jack paused outside the door. "Honey, why don't you four go in. I need to catch my breath and collect my thoughts just a bit."

"Sure thing, Jack," Karen replied. "See you inside in a couple minutes." She kissed him on the cheek and walked into the dining room hand in hand with Jackie, behind Heather and Rob.

Jack exhaled deeply. He turned around, finding himself looking at the large portraits of every American president that lined the walls of the Tenth Corridor directly across from the Executive Dining Room's entrance.

He looked first at President Gore's portrait just to the right of President Rodham, the current occupant of the White House. Jack then scanned back down the line of portraits at the other chief executives who had been his commander-in-chief over the course of his career. He paused briefly at each portrait . . . Kemp, Mondale, Bush, and then Reagan, Carter, Ford, and Nixon. Jack stopped his scan and stared hard at the painting of the "Gipper," thinking how cruel fate had intervened to render the 40th president little more than a very minor footnote in the vast chronicle of American history. Jack's mind raced back to the cold Alaskan day 28 years ago when he'd heard Reagan had been shot - he suddenly remembered how he'd felt that day, and how the nation's budding sense of optimism had seemed to so quickly evaporate after Reagan died.

I wonder, he thought, *if things would have been any different if he'd survived?* He pondered that for a minute, thinking how the forces that shaped history seemed so unalterable and immutable.

Probably not, he rationally concluded, turning around to head into the Executive Dining Room for his retirement luncheon. But as he opened the door to go in, a small part of him still wondered.

AUTHOR'S COMMENTS

This fictional work is based on a straightforward premise, specifically that President Ronald Reagan had as profound an effect on the world we now live in as any leader in the second half of the twentieth century.

As many will remember, Reagan took full advantage of enormous personal popularity and the political power borne of a landslide win over incumbent Jimmy Carter to work his ambitious agenda and vision for America. In particular, he leveraged that popularity and power to persuade a Democratic Congress to back his controversial supply-side economic recovery plan and to match in kind the Soviet defense buildup that had begun in earnest several years earlier under long-time Soviet leader Leonid Brezhnev.

The American business boom of the 1980s and the reconstitution of American military power it helped finance were pivotal to everything that followed. The economic stress of attempting to respond to America's robust defense initiatives helped undermine the already struggling economy of the USSR, which in turn emboldened many behind the Iron Curtain in eastern Europe in ways that would have been unthinkable only a few years earlier. The substantial covert American support of the Mujahadeen rebels fighting the Soviets in Afghanistan also upped the ante and was, to be sure, yet another factor in the calculus that further weakened the Soviet Union.

By the time the first George Bush became President in 1989, the Soviet Union was already rapidly accelerating downward on its hellish slippery slope. President Bush's skillful performance on the world stage during the first two years of his single term – during which time the Wall came down and the nations of Eastern Europe literally rose in unison to achieve independence from Soviet imperial domination – effectively nailed the USSR's coffin shut.

When Saddam Hussein invaded and brutally occupied Kuwait in the late summer of 1990, the Soviet Union was in the very final stages of its death throes. Its economic and military power unthinkably degraded, and beset with insoluble challenges at home and throughout its crumbling empire, the USSR by then had no real ability to influence events and outcomes in the volatile Middle East.

America, on the other hand, did. Unabashedly employing the historically unprecedented freedom of action it now possessed by virtue of its status as the world's sole remaining superpower – at least at that time - America under President Bush cobbled together a truly remarkable global consensus and extraordinary coalition that forcibly ejected Saddam from Kuwait, devastating Iraq's once-formidable military capability in the process.

A year later, the USSR's death rattle finally gurgled forth and the Soviet Union passed into history, replaced by Mother Russia (whose subsequent struggles with indigenous but unruly constituent republics like Chechnya continue to this day) and some fourteen other independent – more or less – new nation states.

The totalitarian government of Saddam, on the other hand, refused to go quietly into the night as many had expected and hoped in the aftermath of the first Gulf War. Instead, his regime managed to survive into the new Millenium by using a remarkably effective skill set of stealth, treachery, brutality, and diplomatic bluster, and by playing on the fears, greed and parochial interests of much of the rest of the world. Not until George Bush the son finally pulled the trigger in March of 2003 did the Baathist Iraqi government finally fall, ultimately driving Saddam into the hole in the ground from which he was ignominiously captured six months later.

In the final analysis, regardless of one's own view of his politics or of the man himself, it seems incontrovertible that Reagan's presidency had a profoundly enormous effect upon the history of this country and this planet over the past several decades. Indeed, Ronald Reagan was arguably the only American politician capable of doing what he did when he did it.

Relevant elements of recent relevant history are catalogued and summarized in the following appendix, to provide readers a quick refresher regarding the specific real-world counterpoints to the story I've told.

JWS

Appendix

The "Real World" 1979-2002

Appendix: The "Real World" 1979-2002

1979

Headline News

SHAH DEPOSED

Pro-American Shah of Iran is overthrown, replaced by Shia leader Ayatollah Khomeini who establishes fundamentalist Islamic government in Iran. Shah flees; new regime executes thousands of government officials and military officers from old regime.

IRANIANS HOLD AMERICANS HOSTAGE

After U.S. allows former Shah to obtain medical treatment in America, Iranian "students" seize U.S. embassy and take around 90 hostages – 52 of them will be held captive for over fourteen months.

SANDINISTAS TRIUMPH

Sandinista rebels in Nicaragua overthrow government of pro-American dictator Anastasio Somoza, who flees and eventually takes sanctuary in Paraguay, where he is assassinated in 1980.

USSR INVADES AFGHANISTAN

The Soviet Union invades and occupies neighboring Afghanistan and orchestrates coup that places supporter Babrak Kamal in power.

MIDEAST PEACE TREATY

Israel and Egypt sign "Camp David peace accords" brokered by President Carter, touching off waves of protest throughout much of the Arab world.

U.S. ECONOMIC DATA – 1979

Inflation 11.2% / Unemployment – 5.8% / Prime Rate – 12.7% / Gas (per gallon) - $0.90

U.S. DEFENSE INDICATORS – 1979

Active Military – 2,031,000 / Defense Budget - $116B, 22.8% of total Federal budget

Appendix: The "Real World" 1979-2002

1980

Headline News

RESCUE MISSION FAILS

U.S. military mission to rescue American hostages in Iran fails with eight Americans killed during the operation. Carter Secretary of State Cyrus Vance resigns in protest; replaced by Senator Edmund Muskie.

IRAN-IRAQ WAR

Iran begins war with neighboring Iran by seizing oil-rich Iranian territory.

OLYMPIC BOYCOTT

President Carter orders American boycott of summer Olympic Games in Moscow in protest of Soviet invasion of Afghanistan.

REAGAN LANDSLIDE

Republican ticket of Ronald Reagan and George H. W. Bush soundly defeat incumbent Democratic President Jimmy Carter and VP Walter Mondale. Carter wins only five states and D.C. Dems maintain control of the House of Representatives (243-192) while GOP gains control of the Senate (53-46) for the first time since 1955.

U.S. ECONOMIC DATA – 1980

Inflation 13.6% / Unemployment – 7.1% / Prime Rate – 15.3% / Gas (per gallon) - $1.25

U.S. DEFENSE INDICATORS – 1980

Active Military – 2,063,000 / Defense Budget - $134B, 22.5% of total Federal budget

Appendix: The "Real World" 1979-2002

1981

Headline News

REAGAN TAKES OFFICE

Ronald Wilson Reagan inaugurated on January 20as 40th President of the United States. All Iran hostages released later same day.

ASSASSINATION ATTEMPT

In late March, John Hinckley, Jr. attempts to assassinate President Reagan outside Hilton Hotel in Washington, D.C. Reagan and three others seriously wounded; all survive, though press secretary James Brady suffers debilitating brain damage.

TAX CUT, DEFENSE INCREASE

Two months after assassination attempt, Reagan unveils economic plan, which includes significant increase in defense spending. Landmark package of tax cuts and non-defense budget reductions is signed into law later that year.

FIRST WOMAN JUSTICE

Reagan appoints Sandra Day O'Connor to the Supreme Court. She is first woman ever appointed to the nation's highest court.

SADAT SLAIN

Egyptian President Anwar Sadat ambushed and killed at military parade in Cairo by assassins wearing military uniforms.

U.S. ECONOMIC DATA – 1981

Inflation 13.6% / Unemployment – 7.1% / Prime Rate – 15.3% / Gas (per gallon) - $1.25

U.S. DEFENSE INDICATORS – 1981

Active Military – 2,101,000 / Defense Budget - $158B, 23% of total Federal budget

Appendix: The "Real World" 1979-2002

1982

Headline News

ISRAEL DRIVES INTO LEBANON

Israeli military forces invade Lebanon, moving quickly into West Beirut and ousting PLO forces of Yasser Arafat, who relocates to Tunisia.

SOVIET LEADER DIES

Leonid Brezhnev, leader of the USSR since 1964, dies at age 75 after several years of ill health. Brezhnev had directed and overseen dramatic increase in Soviet defense spending. Replaced by Yuri Andropov, former head of KGB.

FALKLANDS WAR

Argentina invades and occupies the Falkland Islands in the southern Atlantic. Britain declares war and ejects the occupiers after short but bloody war.

GOP WINS SENATE, DEMS WIN HOUSE

In off-year elections, Republicans increase their majority in the Senate to 54-46. Democrats increase their majority in the House of Representatives to 269-166.

U.S. ECONOMIC DATA – 1982

Inflation 6.2% / Unemployment – 9.7% / Prime Rate – 14.9% / Gas (per gallon) - $1.35

U.S. DEFENSE INDICATORS – 1982

Active Military – 2,130,000 / Defense Budget - $185B, 24.7% of total Federal budget

1983

Headline News

MARINE BARRACKS BOMBED

Terrorist bombing attack in Lebanon kills 241 American marines. U.S. soon thereafter scales back peacekeeping efforts in Lebanon.

ECONOMY REBOUNDS

U.S. economy begins to recover from recession.

"STAR WARS" UNVEILED

President Reagan proposes Strategic Defense Initiative, commonly referred to as "Star Wars," to create defensive ballistic missile shield for American and allies.

GRENADA INVASION

U.S, with the support of the Organization of Eastern Caribbean states, sends combat troops to Grenada in response to recent coup by Communist-leaning Bernard Coard. Although many American allies disapprove of the use of military force, Coard's government is quickly deposed. 19 American troops killed during operation.

U.S. ECONOMIC DATA – 1983

Inflation 3.2% / Unemployment – 9.6% / Prime Rate – 10.8% / Gas (per gallon) - $1.24

U.S. DEFENSE INDICATORS – 1983

Active Military – 2,163,000 / Defense Budget - $219B, 25.4% of total Federal budget

1984

Headline News

ANOTHER BOYCOTT

Soviet bloc nations boycott summer Olympics in Los Angeles, in obvious response to similar American boycott of Moscow games four years earlier.

GANDHI MURDERED

Indian Prime Minister Indira Gandhi assassinated by two of her bodyguards in apparent retaliation for raid she had ordered on sacred Sikh shrine.

STARVATION IN AFRICA

Famine in Ethiopia kills hundreds of thousands.

ANDROPOV SUCCOMBS

Kidney disease kills Yuri Andropov after only 15 months at USSR helm; he is quickly replaced by Konstantin Chernenko.

FOUR MORE YEARS

Reagan and Bush soundly defeat Democratic challengers Walter Mondale and Geraldine Ferraro by 59% to 41% margin – Mondale carries only home state of Minnesota and DC. Democrats retain control of the House (253-182) while GOP keeps majority in Senate (53-47).

JORDAN DRAFTED

After Portland Trailblazers pass him over with second pick of the 1984 NBA draft, Chicago Bulls select Michael Jordan of University of North Carolina. Jordan will lead to six NBA championships, and will be considered by many as the greatest basketball player in history.

U.S. ECONOMIC DATA – 1984

Inflation 4.3% / Unemployment – 7.5% / Prime Rate – 12.0% / Gas (per gallon) - $1.21

U.S. DEFENSE INDICATORS – 1984

Active Military – 2,184,000 / Defense Budget - $227B, 25.9% of total Federal budget

Appendix: The "Real World" 1979-2002

1985

Headline News

GORBACHEV NEW SOVIET LEADER

Mikhail Gorbachev becomes General Secretary of Communist Party of Soviet Union after of General Secretary Chernenko, who succumbs to tuberculosis. Gorbachev soon initiates reforms aimed at invigorating the USSR economy and improving relations with the West.

MORE TAX CUTS

President Reagan unveils new tax program aimed at simplifying tax laws and reducing the maximum tax rates for individuals and corporations.

LEADERS MEET

Reagan and Gorbachev meet for first summit in Washington, DC.

TERROR IN COLUMBIA

Narco-terrorists under the direction of cocaine kingpin Pablo Escobar execute over a hundred hostages, including many judges, during bloody occupation of Palace of Justice in Bogota, Columbia.

ECONOMIC DATA – 1985

Inflation 3.6% / Unemployment – 7.2% / Prime Rate – 9.9% / Gas (per gallon) - $1.20

U.S. DEFENSE INDICATORS – 1985

Active Military – 2,207,000 / Defense Budget - $253B, 25.9% of total Federal budget

1986

Headline News

U.S. BOMBS LIBYA

After linking terrorist bombing at West Berlin disco that killed American GIs to Muammar Gaddafi of Libya, U.S. aircraft attack Tripoli in retaliation. Attack apparently has desired effect, as Libya subsequently scales back support for terrorism.

NUCLEAR DISASTER

Catastrophic accident at Soviet's Chernobyl nuclear power plant causes massive environmental damage in Ukraine and thousands of deaths.

NEW CHIEF JUSTICE

Reagan appoints William Rehnquist as chief justice and Antonin Scalia an associate justice of the Supreme Court.

IRAN-CONTRA SCANDAL

It is disclosed that the U.S. has been selling arms to Iran and using profits to fund Contra forces in Nicaragua. Congress proceeds to publicly investigate.

DEMS TAKE BACK SENATE

Democrats sweep off-year elections, wresting control of the Senate from the GOP, 55-45, and increase majority in House to 258-177.

U.S. ECONOMIC DATA – 1986

Inflation 1.9% / Unemployment – 7.0% / Prime Rate – 8.3% / Gas (per gallon) - $0.93

U.S. DEFENSE INDICATORS – 1986

Active Military – 2,233,000 / Defense Budget - $273B, 26.8% of total Federal budget

1987

Headline News

CONTENTIOUS CONGRESSIONAL HEARINGS

Secretary of Defense Caspar Weinberger, John Poindexter, and Oliver North subpoenaed to testify to Congress regarding Iran-Contra affair.

U.S. NAVAL SHIP ATTACKED

Iraqi missile severely damages USS Stark in the Persian Gulf, killing 30 American sailors. Iraq claims attack was accidental and issues apology.

STOCK MARKET CRASHES

On October 19, what will come to be known as "Black Monday," Wall Street suffers through worst day ever. Dow Jones industrial average loses 23% of its value, dropping over 500 points.

U.S. ECONOMIC DATA – 1987

Inflation 3.7.9% / Unemployment – 6.2% / Prime Rate – 8.23% / Gas (per gallon) - $0.95

U.S. DEFENSE INDICATORS – 1987

Active Military – 2,244,000 / Defense Budget - $282B, 27.3% of total Federal budget

Appendix: The "Real World" 1979-2002

1988

Headline News

IRAN-IRAQ WAR ENDS

After eight years of fighting, Iran-Iraq War ends. Death toll estimated at 1.5 million on both sides.

SOVIETS LEAVE EUROPE

In what is clearly a cost-cutting measure, Gorbachev announces that USSR will reduce military presence in eastern Europe by half a million troops.

ANOTHER NEW JUSTICE

Making his fourth nomination to fill a Supreme Court seat, Reagan appoints Anthony Kennedy to become associate justice.

JORDAN CEDES WEST BANK TO PLO

Jordan's King Hussein renounces control of West Bank, ceding former Jordanian territory to Palestine Liberation Organization.

BUSH ELECTED PRESIDENT

George H. W. Bush and Dan Quayle defeat Democratic challengers Michael Dukakis and Lloyd Bentsen. Dems retain control of the Senate, 55-45, and House, 258-177.

U.S. ECONOMIC DATA – 1988

Inflation 4.1% / Unemployment – 5.5% / Prime Rate – 9.3% / Gas (per gallon) - $0.95

U.S. DEFENSE INDICATORS – 1988

Active Military – 2,209,000 / Defense Budget - $290B, 26.5% of total Federal budget

Appendix: The "Real World" 1979-2002

1989

Headline News

BUSH NEW PRESIDENT

George H. W. Bush inaugurated 41st U.S. President.

TIANANMEN SQUARE

Thousands of students occupy Tiananmen Square in Beijing to demand democracy in China, precipitating internal government struggle. Hardliners prevail; military forcibly puts down protest.

SOVIETS DEPART AFGHANISTAN

USSR military forces withdraw from Afghanistan after nearly a decade. Soviets lose estimated 16,000 troops killed in action.

COMMUNISM FALLS IN RUSSIA AND EUROPE

USSR conducts free elections. Communist governments in Poland, Czechoslovakia, Romania, and East Germany all fall. Berlin Wall, which had divided the city for almost three decades, is dismantled piece by piece by jubilant Berliners on both sides of city.

U.S. INVADES PANAMA

After months of increasing tensions, U.S. invades Panama, overthrowing regime of strongman Manuel Noriega. Noriega surrenders after first taking refuge in Papal Nuncio in Panama City. 23 Americans killed during operations.

U.S. ECONOMIC DATA – 1989

Inflation 4.8% / Unemployment – 5.3% / Prime Rate – 10.9% / Gas (per gallon) - $1.02

U.S. DEFENSE INDICATORS – 1989

Active Military – 2,203,000 / Defense Budget - $304B, 25.8% of total Federal budget

1990

Headline News

IRAQ INVADES KUWAIT

After weeks of escalating tensions, Iraq invades and occupies Emirate of Kuwait. Emir escapes to Saudi Arabia, but brother is killed by Iraqi forces. Iraq dictator Saddam Hussein declares Kuwait an Iraqi province.

U.S. CONFERS WITH SAUDI KING

Secretary of Defense Cheney and USCENTCOM commander General Schwarzkopf meet with King Fahd in Riyadh and convince him to allow American military forces into Saudi Arabia to defend against Iraqi threat.

BALTIC INDEPENDENCE

Lithuanian parliament declares its independence from USSR, followed shortly by Baltic neighbors Latvia and Estonia.

YELTSIN ELECTED IN RUSSIA

Boris Yeltsin, having renounced his membership in the Communist Party, is elected President of Russian Federation.

GERMAN REUNIFICATION

East and West Germany formally reunify, ending the forced division of Germany imposed by the Allies and the end of World War II.

YUGOSLAVIA BREAKUP BEGINS

Yugoslavian Communist Party votes to give up exclusive governing power, declaring country a "multi-party democracy." Slovenia and Croatia regions elect governments favoring independence; Serbia, on the other hand, elects party committed to keeping Yugoslavia intact.

NEW SUPREME COURT JUSTICE

President Bush makes his first appointment to Supreme Court, appointing David Souter as associate justice.

SANDINISTAS LOSE ELECTION

In Nicaraguan nation election, opposition led by former La Prensa editor defeats Sandinista President Daniel Ortega.

DEMS RETAIN CONTROL OF CONGRESS

In off-year election, Democrats retain firm control of both House (267-167) and Senate (56-44).

U.S. ECONOMIC DATA – 1990

Inflation 5.4% / Unemployment – 5.6% / Prime Rate – 10.0% / Gas (per gallon) - $1.16

U.S. DEFENSE INDICATORS – 1990

Active Military – 2,144,000 / Defense Budget - $299B, 23.1% of total Federal budget

Appendix: The "Real World" 1979-2002

1991

Headline News

DESERT STORM

American and coalition military forcibly eject Iraqi forces from Kuwait during operation Desert Storm, decimating much of Saddam Hussein's military.

MORE NUKE REDUCTIONS

START I Treaty is signed by Bush and Gorbachev mandating additional reductions in U.S. and Russian nuclear arsenals.

CONTROVERSIAL NEW JUSTICE

President Bush names Clarence Thomas as associate justice of the Supreme Court. After contentious Senate hearing centering on allegations of sexual harassment, Thomas is confirmed.

SOVIET COUP ATTEMPT, USSR DISINTEGRATES

A coup attempt by hardliners attempts to bring down government of Mikhail Gorbachev, placing him under house arrest. The coup attempt quickly collapses when Boris Yeltsin rallies opposition to takeover. Coup-plotters arrested, and Gorbachev outlaws Communist Party. Not long after, the Soviet Union is dissolved, replaced by 15 separate nations.

BASE CLOSURES, U.S. NUCLEAR FORCES STAND DOWN

Congress approves recommendation for closure of over two dozen American military bases. Meanwhile, President Bush announces that all U.S. nuclear weapons will be removed from Europe, and stands down Strategic Command from 24-hour alert status it had maintained throughout Cold War.

U.S. ECONOMIC DATA – 1991

Inflation 4.3% / Unemployment – 6.8% / Prime Rate – 8.5% / Gas (per gallon) - $1.14

U.S. DEFENSE INDICATORS – 1991

Active Military – 2,077,000 / Defense Budget - $273B, 19.8% of total Federal budget

Appendix: The "Real World" 1979-2002

1992

Headline News

YUGOSLAVIA FLIES APART

Civil war breaks out in Yugoslavia, as Bosnia, Macedonia, Croatia, and Slovenia seek independence. Serbia forcibly attempts to gain control of country, instituting "ethnic cleansing" of areas under Serb control.

ARAFAT PLANE CRASH

Palestinian leader Yasir Arafat seriously injured in plane crash in Libya.

SAC DISESTABLISHED

The Air Force's vaunted Strategic Air Command (SAC), responsible for the nation's nuclear bombers and land-based ICBMs, is disestablished.

LIBYA SANCTIONS

UN Security Council votes sanction on Libya for surrendering suspects in the deadly bombing of a Pan Am flight over Scotland.

PEACE IN EL SALVADOR

Government and rebels sign peace treaty in El Salvador, ending 13-year civil war.

CLINTON WINS PRESIDENCY

Democrat ticket of Bill Clinton and Albert Gore only collect 43% of the popular vote, but nevertheless defeat incumbent President Bush and VP Quayle when independent candidate Ross Perot garners almost 19% of the vote. Dems retain control of the House (258-176) and Senate (57-43).

U.S. ECONOMIC DATA – 1992

Inflation 3.0% / Unemployment – 7.5% / Prime Rate – 6.3% / Gas (per gallon) - $1.13

U.S. DEFENSE INDICATORS – 1992

Active Military – 1,880,000 / Defense Budget - $298B, 20.7% of total Federal budget

Appendix: The "Real World" 1979-2002

1993

Headline News

MORE NUKE REDUCTIONS

President Bush and Russian President Yeltsin sign START II Treaty to cut nuclear warheads by two thirds by 2003.

CLINTON TAKES OFFICE

William Jefferson Clinton of Arkansas inaugurated as 42nd President of United States. Albert Gore of Tennessee becomes VP.

TERROR ATTACK IN NYC

Powerful car bomb in underground garage rocks World Trade Center in New York City, killing seven and injuring over 1,000. Several Muslim radicals later convicted for attack.

WACO STANDOFF

After a 51-day standoff following the deaths of four ATF agents in February, federal agents raid a compound near Waco, Texas occupied by David Koresh and his Branch Davidian follows. Over 80 sect members, including Koresh, die.

GAY CONTROVERSY

Political firestorm erupts when President Clinton announces he'll permit gays to serve openly in the military. Congress disagree, enacts "Don't Ask, Don't Tell."

SECOND WOMAN TO COURT

Clinton nominates Ruth Bader Ginsburg to Supreme Court, second woman ever appointed.

AMERICAN SOLDIERS DIE IN SOMALIA

Eighteen U.S. soldiers participating in United Nations peace-keeping mission in Somalia are killed in battle with rebels in Mogadishu. U.S. subsequently withdraws most troops.

MORE BASE CLOSURES

In second round of U.S. military base closures, 30 more installations are axed.

U.S. ECONOMIC DATA – 1993

Inflation 3.0% / Unemployment – 6.9% / Prime Rate – 6.0% / Gas (per gallon) - $1.11

U.S. DEFENSE INDICATORS – 1993

Active Military – 1,755,000 / Defense Budget - $291B, 19.8% of total Federal budget

Appendix: The "Real World" 1979-2002

1994

Headline News

CIVIL WAR IN CHECHNYA

Conflict breaks out after Russia rejects demand from province of Chechnya for independence. Russan military forces will battle Chechnyan rebels for two years in bloody civil war.

NATO FIGHTS IN YUGOSLAVIA

In first combat in its 45-year history, NATO forces shoot down Serbian aircraft in UN mandated "no fly zone" in former Republic of Yugoslavia.

BACK TO IRAQ

When Saddam Hussein masses forces in threatening manner near Kuwait border, U.S. hurriedly moves more troops and aircraft into region during Operation Vigilant Warrior. Iraq "blinks" and withdraws troops from border.

REPUBLICANS SWEEP OFF-YEAR ELECTION

Republicans take control of both houses of Congress, with a 230-204 majority in the House of Representatives and a 52-48 majority in the Senate.

U.S. ECONOMIC DATA – 1994

Inflation 2.6% / Unemployment – 6.1% / Prime Rate – 7.2% / Gas (per gallon) - $1.11

U.S. DEFENSE INDICATORS – 1994

Active Military – 1,678,000 / Defense Budget - $282B, 18.4% of total Federal budget

1995

Headline News

MEXICAN BAILOUT

Invoking emergency powers, President Clinton grants $20 billion to Mexico after collapse of the peso. Mexico repays loan early.

OKLAHOMA CITY BOMBING

Massive truck bomb explodes in front of Murrah Federal Building in Oklahoma City, killing 168 and injuring many more in worst act of terror ever on American soil to date. Gulf War vet Timothy MacVeigh will be executed six years later after being convicted of attack.

ISRAELI PM MURDERED

Israeli Prime Minister Yitzhak Rabin assassinated by right wing opponent of peace process. Succeeded by Foreign Minister Shimon Peres.

YUGOSLAVIA FIGHTING ENDS

Serbia, Bosnia, and Croatia sign treaty ending war that has killed 20,000 in the former Yugoslavia.

BASE CLOSURES CONTINUE

Pentagon announces third round of military base closures.

TRUCE IN CHECHNYA

Russia and breakaway republic of Chechnya agree to truce in conflict that has already killed 25,000.

MARKET WAY UP

Dow Jones ends year at 5117.2, an increase of 33% over past twelve months.

U.S. ECONOMIC DATA – 1995

Inflation 2.8% / Unemployment – 5.6% / Prime Rate 8.8% / Gas (per gallon) - $1.15

U.S. DEFENSE INDICATORS – 1995

Active Military – 1,583,000 / Defense Budget - $272B, 17.2% of total Federal budget

Appendix: The "Real World" 1979-2002

1996

Headline News

TRUCK BOMB KILLS GIs IN SAUDI ARABIA

A powerful truck bomb explodes outside the perimeter of the Khobar Towers military housing area in near Dhahran, Saudi Arabia. 19 American personnel are killed, and many more injured.

TALIBAN TAKE AFGHANISTAN

Taliban capture Kabul and ruthlessly enforce their strict interpretation of Islamic law throughout most of Afghanistan. Opposition groups in north of country unite in attempt to oppose Taliban rule.

YELTSIN RE-ELECTED

After a difficult and frequently bitter political campaign, Russian President Boris Yeltsin is re-elected for a second term.

CLINTON WINS, GOP KEEPS CONGRESS

President Clinton and VP Gore easily defeat GOP ticket of Robert Dole and Jack Kemp, winning 31 states and amassing an 8.5% margin of victory in popular voting. Republicans retain control of House (226-207) and increase their majority in the Senate to 55-45.

U.S. ECONOMIC DATA – 1996

Inflation 2.9% / Unemployment – 5.6% / Prime Rate – 8.3% / Gas (per gallon) - $1.23

U.S. DEFENSE INDICATORS – 1996

Active Military – 1,538,000 / Defense Budget - $266B, 16.2% of total Federal budget

Appendix: The "Real World" 1979-2002

1997

Headline News

BRITISH RULE OF HONG KONG ENDS

Great Britain's long-standing control of Hong Kong ends peacefully, as the British transfer sovereignty over their former colony to China.

IRAQ EXPELS UN INSPECTORS

Ignoring the provisions of the agreement that ended the Gulf War six years earlier, Saddam Hussein expels United Nations inspectors attempting to confirm that Iraq has dismantled its weapons of mass destruction.

RWANDA CIVIL WAR

Ethnic violence between Hutus and Tutsis ravages Rwanda, escalating into full civil war.

BULL MARKET CONTINUES

Despite a temporary decline during Asian market crisis, Dow Jones rises 20% during year, the third straight to achieve at least that level of growth.

U.S. ECONOMIC DATA – 1997

Inflation 2.3% / Unemployment – 4.9% / Prime Rate – 8.4% / Gas (per gallon) - $1.23

U.S. DEFENSE INDICATORS – 1997

Active Military – 1,504,000 / Defense Budget - $271B, 16.1% of total Federal budget

Appendix: The "Real World" 1979-2002

1998

Headline News

TERROR BOMBINGS AT AMERICAN EMBASSIES

Terrorist bombs detonate simultaneously at American embassies in Kenya and Tanzania, killing 224. U.S. quickly determines attack is work of Al Qaeda terrorist organization led by Osama Bin Laden. In response, President Clinton orders cruise missile attacks of suspected terrorist targets in Afghanistan and Sudan.

RUSSIAN ECONOMIC WOES

With ruble devalued, international loans unpaid, and incomes dropping, Russia experiences worst economic year since collapse of USSR.

AIR STRIKES AGAINST IRAQ

U.S. and Britain launch bombing strikes against Iraq in response to Iraq failure to cooperate with UN inspections.

GOP KEEPS BOTH HOUSES

In off-year elections, Republicans maintain control of the House by a 223-211 majority and the Senate by 55-45 margin.

U.S. ECONOMIC DATA – 1998

Inflation 1.6% / Unemployment – 4.5% / Prime Rate – 8.4% / Gas (per gallon) - $1.06

U.S. DEFENSE INDICATORS – 1998

Active Military – 1,470,000 / Defense Budget - $268B, 15.5% of total Federal budget

Appendix: The "Real World" 1979-2002

1999

Headline News

KOSOVO BOMBING CAMPAIGN

After brutal Serbian ethnic cleansing activities in province of Kosovo, U.S. and NATO forces conduct intensive bombing campaign against Serbian military targets and forces. After 79 days, Serbia capitulates and withdraws forces from Kosovo.

YELTSIN BOWS OUT

Russian President Boris Yeltsin resigns and names Prime Minister Vladimir Putin to succeed him.

CLINTON IMPEACHMENT

President Clinton, accused of lying to a grand jury and giving false testimony in a civil lawsuit, is impeached by the House of Representatives in a straight party-line vote. After a trial in the Senate, only 50 senators vote to find him guilty, well short of the 66 votes needed to convict and remove him from office.

CHECHNYA REIGNITES

For the second time this decade, Russian military forces launch major offensive against separatist guerillas in breakaway republic of Chechnya.

PANAMA NOW CONTROLS CANAL

As year ends, Panama takes control of the Panama Canal from the U.S. as per treaty negotiated during the Carter administration two decades earlier.

U.S. ECONOMIC DATA – 1999

Inflation 2.2% / Unemployment – 4.2% / Prime Rate – 8.0% / Gas (per gallon) - $1.17

U.S. DEFENSE INDICATORS – 1999

Active Military 1,451,000 / Defense Budget - $275B, 15.4% of total Federal budget

Appendix: The "Real World" 1979-2002

2000

Headline News

PUTIN ELECTED

Vladimir Putin is formally elected President of Russia. Some fear a return to expansionism and authoritarianism.

SYRIAN PRESIDENT DIES

After almost 30 years in office, Syria's Baathist President Hafez al-Assad dies at 69. Was implacable foe of Israel.

MARKET TUMBLES

NASDAQ, America's high tech stock index, declines 39% during 2000, its worst performance ever.

BUSH WINS PRESIDENCY

After the Supreme Court votes 5-4 to end the controversial Florida recount process, George W. Bush is finally declared president-elect. Although Bush and his running mate Dick Cheney narrowly lose the national popular vote to Democrats Al Gore and Joe Lieberman, the Republican ticket wins the electoral vote contest 271-266. Republican control of the House shrinks to 221-212, while the Senate will now be split 50-50 between the GOP and Dems.

U.S. ECONOMIC DATA – 2000

Inflation 3.4% / Unemployment – 4.0% / Prime Rate – 9.2% / Gas (per gallon) - $1.51

U.S. DEFENSE INDICATORS – 2000

Active Military – 1,449,000 / Defense Budget - $294B, 15.7% of total Federal budget

Appendix: The "Real World" 1979-2002

2001

Headline News

BUSH INAUGURATED

George Walker Bush becomes 43rd President of the United States.

TAX CUT

In first significant tax cut since the Reagan administration, President Bush signs tax bill that calls for $1.35 trillion tax cut over next ten years.

SEPTEMBER 11

In a skillfully coordinated terror attack orchestrated by Al Qaeda, two hijacked airliners strike and bring down the twin towers of the World Trade Center in New York City, and another strikes the Pentagon in Washington, DC. A fourth hijacked airliner, apparently also headed for the nation's capital, crashes in Pennsylvania when passengers heroically fight back. Nearly 3,000 die in worst terror attack ever on American soil.

ANTHRAX SCARE

Shortly after 9/11 attacks, powdered anthrax is discovered in letters addressed to major media outlets and government official. Five deaths result.

OPERATION ENDURING FREEDOM

After Taliban regime in Afghanistan refuses to hand over leaders of Al Qaeda, a U.S. led multinational coalition begins a major military operation to overthrow Taliban government. By year's end, Afghan resistance and coalition forces have routed the Taliban and greatly disrupted Al Qaeda operations. Efforts to quickly kill or capture Bin Laden, however, are not successful. It would be another ten years before American special forces would be able to locate Bin Laden and eliminate him.

U.S. ECONOMIC DATA – 2001

Inflation 2.8% / Unemployment – 4.7% / Prime Rate – 6.9% / Gas (per gallon) - $1.46

U.S. DEFENSE INDICATORS – 2001

Active Military – 1,451,000 / Defense Budget - $306B, 15.6% of total Federal budget

Appendix: The "Real World" 1979-2002

2002

Headline News

WAR ON TERROR CONTINUES

U.S. bombing raids and special operation missions in Afghanistan continue against Al Qaeda terrorists. Hundreds of captured detainees are transported to hastily built confinement facility at Guantanamo Bay, Cuba.

KARZAI NEW AFGHAN LEADER

Hamid Karzai is officially elected as head of state of Afghanistan. Sporadic fighting continues involving remnants of Taliban regime, Al Qaeda, and others opposed to new government.

MIDDLE EAST VIOLENCE ESCALATES

In a year marked by continuing violence on both sides, Israeli-Palestinian conflict threatens to escalate out of control.

WEAPONS INSPECTORS RETURN TO IRAQ

UN weapons inspectors return to Iraq while U.S. considers military action to topple government of Saddam Hussein.

GOP WINS BIG

In off-year election, Republicans surprisingly increase majority in both House (228-205) and Senate (51.48).

U.S. ECONOMIC DATA – 2002

Inflation 1.6% / Unemployment – 5.8% / Prime Rate – 4.7% / Gas (per gallon) - $1.36

U.S. DEFENSE INDICATORS – 2002

Active Military – 1,478,000 / Defense Budget - $349B, 15.5% of total Federal budget

APPENDIX Data Sources

- Defense Indicator Data extracted from tables 7-1, 7-6, and 7-7 of the *National Defense Budget Estimates for 2004* submission by the Office of the Undersecretary of Defense (Comptroller), March 2003.
- Inflation data from

http://inflationdata.com/inflation/inflation_rate/

- Unemployment data from

http://www.economagic.com/em-cgi-/data.exe/blsin/inu0022us0

- Average retail gas price data extracted from DOE Web Page

http://www.eia.doe.gov/emeu/aer/petro.html

- Prime Rate data from Federal Reserve Webpage

http://www.federalreserve.gov/releases/h15/data/a/prime.txt

About the Author

Jim Swanson is a former military lawyer and a retired USAF brigadier general.

He grew up in Mundelein, Illinois, north of Chicago, and entered the Air Force following his graduation from Purdue University with a BA degree in journalism. He was later selected by the Air Force to attend law school, earning a *Juris Doctorate* from the University of Illinois.

He spent most of his Air Force career as a judge advocate, serving in a variety of legal and military management positions around the world, including several deployments to the Middle East. He retired after 32 years active-duty service.

After his retirement from the military, he served in a number of executive and management positions, including as a member of the senior executive service (SES) with the Department of Homeland Security, general counsel and corporate secretary to the Military Officers Association of America, Senior Director heading the

American Bar Association's large Washington, DC office, and as CEO of a charitable non-profit in Naples, FL.

Printed in the USA
CPSIA information can be obtained
at www.ICGtesting.com
LVHW092343221023
761838LV00005B/116